Rachel Bird

RACHEL BIRD

BECKY CITRA

Second Story Press

Library and Archives Canada Cataloguing in Publication

Title: Rachel Bird / Becky Citra.
Names: Citra, Becky, author.
Identifiers: Canadiana (print) 20210301708 | Canadiana (ebook)
   20210301724 | ISBN 9781772602432 (softcover) | ISBN
   9781772602449 (EPUB)
Classification: LCC PS8555.I87 R33 2022 | DDC jC813/.54—dc23

Cover photo: iStock.com/den-belitsky

Editor: Heather Tekavec

Printed and bound in Canada

*Second Story Press gratefully acknowledges the support of the
Ontario Arts Council and the Canada Council for the Arts for our
publishing program. We acknowledge the financial support of the
Government of Canada through the Canada Book Fund.*

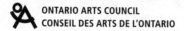

Published by
SECOND STORY PRESS
20 Maud Street, Suite 401
Toronto, ON M5V 2M5
www.secondstorypress.ca

To Larry and Meghan and the life we share on our ranch.

CHAPTER ONE

Aleksandra dropped us off half an hour ago for our last coun-selling session. Jane's sitting in the little kids' corner, coloring a frog with a broken orange crayon. Usually we talk to Aura separately but today we're here mostly just to say good-bye. I slide lower in my chair and examine my toenails. I'm wearing pink flip-flops. Maybe I'll walk downtown when we get back and buy some blue nail polish. I'll do Jane's toes, too.

"Hey," says Aura. "Earth to Rachel."

Aura wears glasses with heavy black frames. A tattoo of a Celtic knot covers the top of her right arm. It's like a loop with no start and finish and it represents eternity. Aura's tattoo is called a triquetra or trinity knot. I'm considering a Celtic knot when I get a tattoo, but mine will be different. I've been googling them.

Aura was helping Jane with her coloring but now she's

sitting on a huge blue ball opposite me. She calls it "active sitting" because it makes her core stronger. She's wearing jeans with ripped knees. There's a bowl of goldfish crackers on a little table.

"Got something for you," she says.

She scoots over to her desk, opens a drawer, and takes out a pair of sunglasses.

"Right," I say. They look like something Uncle Rob would wear, not me.

"They're not just *ordinary* sunglasses," she says. "They cancel out blue light so you can look at screens in the evening without wrecking your sleep."

Aura knows that I don't text friends all night long in between posting on Facebook. Every time I move, I leave my friends behind. But she also knows I'm a little addicted to googling things.

"They won't work," I say.

"I got a pair for me, too."

They *won't* work. "Okay. Thanks."

I tuck the sunglasses into my backpack and glance at the clock on the wall. Aura's leaving for Europe in three days with her boyfriend, Mike. I refuse to start over again with someone new. So, this is the end of counselling for me and Jane.

I stand up.

"Sit down, Rach," says Aura.

I sit.

"We've covered a lot of stuff you and me," she says.

"Yeah."

She hands me a tissue.

"I get how hard this is. I think you've made a lot of progress. And I really appreciate how honest you've been with me."

I can't trust my voice, so I don't say anything.

"Do you know what a carapace is?" she says.

"Nope."

"It's the hard upper shell of a turtle, crustacean, or arachnid." She smiles. "I bet you know where I'm going with this."

"You think I'm a turtle."

"No, but I do think you've built a protective shell around yourself. It's a pretty common coping strategy. What do you think?"

"I don't know."

"Your Uncle Rob really loves you and Jane. Don't forget that. He's your ally. And your grandparents, too."

So much for Aleksandra being part of this. Aura's got her figured out. She slides off the ball. "Okay. Group hug. Come on, Jane."

Jane scampers over and wraps her skinny arms around Aura's waist.

"I'm going to miss you guys, big time," says Aura. "You look after yourselves this summer and I'll see you in the fall."

After Europe, she and Mike are trekking all over Asia. Aura's awesome, but seriously? Why would she want to spend all summer listening to the problems of kids that aren't even hers? She'll eat sushi and see the Great Wall of China. She'll never come back. I wouldn't.

~

Aleksandra's waiting at the end of the block in her bright red Mini Cooper. She's double parked and she taps the horn when she sees us. Jane squeezes into the back and I slide into the passenger seat, fitting my long legs around a gym bag and a paper sack of groceries.

Aleksandra zips into the traffic. "So, what did you and Aura talk about today, Jane?" she says.

"Well," says Jane. "We didn't talk about Mom."

"What!" says Aleksandra. "Why not?"

"I don't know."

"What did you talk about?"

"I don't know." Jane bangs her runners against the back of my seat. "Can we have hot dogs for dinner?"

"Ouch," I say. "Quit that."

Aleksandra runs a red light and a horn blasts. "No hot dogs. I picked up some fresh cod and asparagus at Granville Island Market."

"Oh Gaaawd," says Jane.

I laugh and Aleksandra frowns in the rearview mirror. "Rachel? What did *you* talk about?"

She's determined that she and Uncle Rob get their money's worth from Aura.

"Nose rings," I say.

She sighs and flips on the radio.

~

It's scorching by the time we get back to the apartment, so I forget the idea of trudging all the way downtown to get nail polish. Instead, I grab our bathing suits, towels, and library books and stuff everything in my backpack.

Aleksandra's on her phone, swearing at someone in Polish because they're telling her for the millionth time that she can't practice medicine in Canada with a Polish license. "We're going!" I yell, and she flaps her hand in the air.

She and Uncle Rob are renting this apartment in the West End while they look for a condo to buy. Jane and I have been living here since Christmas. Six months. An all-time record. It's better than anywhere we've ever lived before. Stanley Park is right outside the window. You can smell the ocean and it's seven minutes to the pool at Second Beach.

We walk to the library on shady streets with tall leafy trees. I leave Jane in the children's section and head to *Young Adults* with a list Aura gave me: *26 Young Adult Fantasy Novels You Need to Read.*

I have a system when I pick out my library books. It's random. Last week, I took out books with one-word titles. Today, I'm looking for books with the word *blood* in the title.

I find *Children of Blood and Bone* by Tomi Adeyemi, *Bloodwitch* by Susan Dennard, and *The Blood Spell* by CJ Redevine. Then I break my rule and grab *Lady Smoke* by Laura Sebastian because I love the way it sounds.

Lady Smoke. When I come back in my next life, I'm going to call myself Lady Smoke.

Jane has a stack of *Magic Treehouse* books. There's got to be at least fifty books in the series and she's on her second time through. I taught her to read when she was three. The librarian adores her and gives her a high five as we leave.

One more stop before we go swimming—the West End Community Center next door to the library, to pick up a brochure. We scan it together, searching for activities that Jane can do this summer.

"Okay," I say. "Kid Zone, Lego Block Party, Star Wars Day, Seeds and Senses, Thumb Print Art, Bee an Eco Hero."

"All that?" says Jane.

"Yup. It'll be fun."

I love taking care of Jane. We've always stuck together. But I have stuff to do. I'm looking for someone. And he's not going to be at Thumb Print Art.

CHAPTER TWO

Jane and I hang around the pool at Second Beach all afternoon. Unlike me (red hair, pale skin—it's so unjust), Jane gets darker and darker, but I've slathered her with sunscreen anyway. Now she's hunched up on her towel near the little kids' seal slide, hugging her knees. She gets cold even on a hot day and once she starts, she can't stop shivering. She's probably starving, too.

I wave and she waves back.

A moment later, I'm standing over her, my long, wet hair dripping on her head. She wriggles away. "Can I get some mac and cheese bites? Please, please, please?"

At the concession stand, I order the mac and cheese bites, and we refill our water bottles at the drinking fountain while we wait. I have an apple and an orange in my backpack. I don't eat at concession stands.

I carry the little cardboard box of mac and cheese bites,

so they won't spill, and we walk down the cement stairs to the beach. People are everywhere, stretched out on towels and baking in the sun, splashing in and out of the ocean. Somewhere music is blaring. We find an empty log, kick off our flip-flops, and bury our toes in the sand. I count five huge orange freighters as a sailboat with white sails skims across the water.

"Are you meeting those guys again?" says Jane. She's wrapped up in my towel because she's still shivering.

"Nope." But my eyes drift up and down the beach.

I've seen them here three times, two girls and three guys, playing Frisbee and hanging out. They've just finished grade nine at King George Secondary. I know them from my math class.

Last time, one of the guys, Jason, tossed the Frisbee at me and then they all wandered over.

Caitlin, a gorgeous volleyball star who can't do multiplication, smiled at Jane. "Hey, look at that little girl! She's reading a book at the beach. That's adorable!"

Jane scowled, then she rolled over on her stomach and her towel slipped off. Caitlin's mouth fell open and I knew she was staring at Jane's arm. Then she looked at me and I drilled my eyes back at her until she turned red.

Everyone flopped down on the sand and talked mostly about the teachers they hated and their lousy report cards.

"Old Turco is out to get me.... Try having Mr. B for history. He's a moron.... I flunked History and Science. God. I'll have to go to summer school."

I didn't contribute, but no one seemed to notice. I knew NOT to:

1. take my library book out of my backpack and read

2. confess that I got straight As in English, Social Studies, and French

Jason wasn't saying anything either. He's new at King George. He appeared about a month ago. His eyes are very dark and he's always tossing his long black hair off his face.

While the others talked, he flicked bits of broken shells at my leg. When they left, he said super casually, "We're coming back tomorrow."

I haven't tried to make any friends at King George. Now it's almost the summer holidays and I'm regretting it. I'm sick of being the girl whose mother died. I want someone to hang out with. And I'm pretty sure Jason was giving me a signal.

I went back to the beach last week, even to the same log, without Jane. But they never showed up. Maybe I was too late. Or too early. Or maybe it wasn't a signal at all.

One last look around. They aren't coming today either.

"Can I get some Twizzlers?" says Jane.

~

We go for a walk along the seawall so Jane can read the sayings on the memorial benches. She's memorized six benches, which so far is the farthest we've walked. Her favorite is,

Do not complain about the rain.
Think of all the raindrops that are missing you.

She laughs every time. If I died and someone wrote that on a bench to remember me, I'd come back to haunt them.

"I got one," I say. "Lady Smoke. She evaporated into thin air."

"Can a person evaporate?" says Jane.

"Lady Smoke can. Just like that! Poof!"

The first time Jane talked about the memorial benches at the dinner table, Aleksandra said, "Do you think that's a good idea…well, considering…. Really, Rob, memorial benches?"

We do three more benches today. We agree that *I love you to the moon and back* is the best.

"I love you to Mars and back," I say.

"I love you to Jupiter and back," says Jane.

Why did I start this? Now she has to go through every planet. She's on to asteroids when I say, "C'mon. Let's go."

We double back to Stanley Park and duck through a short concrete tunnel, over a bridge, and onto the path by the tennis courts. Two more minutes and we're at the apartment on Comox Street.

Uncle Rob's in the kitchen talking to Aleksandra. The door's partly open. As I dump my backpack on the floor and start pulling out the wet towels, Aleksandra says, "You're going to have to tell them soon."

"Shh," I say to Jane.

"I know," says Uncle Rob. "It's just that—"

"I didn't sign up for this, Rob," says Aleksandra. "We agreed. Focus on our careers. No kids."

"You could give them a break, Aleks."

"I do. But I can't deal with it anymore. Not right now."

She gives this huge dramatic sigh. That's very Aleksandra. "I can handle Rachel, although she completely ignores her curfews. And the way she skulks around in the dark is disturbing. The other night I got up to get a drink of water and she was sitting on the couch at two a.m. with a blanket over her head."

I love you too, Aleksandra.

"Jane is something else," she says. "She won't eat anything I cook."

I put my hand on Jane's shoulder.

"She's six," says Uncle Rob.

"A six-year-old shouldn't wet her bed every night. And she doesn't talk like any six-year-old that I've ever met."

"Not every night," I whisper to Jane. "And you talk way smarter."

"I can't do this anymore," says Aleksandra.

"Okay, okay, I'll send them," says Uncle Rob. "As soon as school's done. But you've got to promise it's only for the summer."

"I won't promise that."

"Where is he sending us?" Jane sounds shaky.

"I think it's Aspen Lake." I poke her in the ribs. "Don't worry. We're not going."

CHAPTER THREE

After supper, Uncle Rob takes Jane and me to the Marble Slab Creamery on Denman Street. This is how it works: you order your flavor of ice cream, and they scoop it onto a marble slab and mix in toppings that you pick from little plastic boxes. Then they scrape the entire mess into a cone.

Jane picks bubble gum ice cream. She asks the girl behind the counter to add mini marshmallows, chocolate chips, M&Ms, gummy bears, Nerds, coconut, and sprinkles. I choose vanilla. One small scoop. No toppings.

We take our cones to a table in the corner where Uncle Rob is cradling a coffee from Starbucks. He eyes Jane's cone, which is collapsing under its load, and shoves a handful of napkins across the table.

"Okay. This is the deal."

I lick my ice cream slowly.

"Aleksandra's been under a lot of stress fighting this bureaucracy. Trying to find ways to get around all the obstacles."

Jane's digging out all the gummy bears and piling them up to eat at the end.

"What does that mean?" she says without looking up.

"It means she really wants to be a doctor here in Canada, like she was in Poland. But the government won't let her. Even though she's married to me, and I'm a Canadian citizen."

"Why?"

"It's just the rules. But it's very frustrating."

"Are you going to go back to Poland?" Jane glances up now. Her mouth is circled in blue and there's chocolate on her chin.

"No. That's not an option. Not…now."

"That's because you have to look after me and Rachel."

"Well, yes. And your grandparents need me too. It was just time for me to come home."

I decide to enter this conversation. "So, Aleksandra's under a lot of stress and…what?"

"I talked to your grandmother last night and she thinks… *we* think it would be a good idea for you to go to Aspen Lake for a while." Uncle Rob caves in the sides of his coffee cup and tosses it on the table. "Actually, for the summer."

"You mean Margaret who phones us every Sunday?" says Jane.

"Yes. Your grandmother."

Uncle Rob discussed possible names with us last December. Did we like Grandma and Grandpa, Granny and Grandad? I suggested Pops and Bunny. Jane was in agony trying to decide.

At the end, it didn't matter. The tall pale woman with a gray braid who came up to us at the funeral home said, "Hello. You must be Rachel and Jane. I'm Margaret. Wayne isn't well enough to come but he sends his love."

Can't get more definite than that.

Uncle Rob goes to Aspen Lake all the time. He often drives there on a Friday night and comes back late Sunday. He's always tired and irritable when he gets home and he's never suggested taking us. And he never talks about what he does there.

"Your grandparents are very keen for you to come for a visit," he says. "They want to get to know you. You'll love it. You'll be staying in the same house where your mom and Uncle Jimmy and I grew up. It's a real ranch. There's horses and a lake to swim in. It'll be fantastic."

I know how this works. We all bond and live happily ever after.

Jane studies my face.

"I actually prefer sidewalks," I say. "And lampposts. And… um, let's see. Oh yeah. Traffic lights."

Jane frowns. Then she turns to Uncle Rob. "Okay. I'll go."

"You're a trooper. Rachel?"

I look away and spot Jason through the window, waiting to cross the street. He's holding a skateboard and he's not with his usual group. If he turns left, that'll put him on a direct route to the Marble Slab Creamery.

I jump up. "Gotta go."

"Now?" says Uncle Rob. "Where?"

"I'll be home by my curfew. And thanks for the ice cream."

~

"Hey! Rachel!"

"Oh! Hey."

"Where are you going so fast?" Jason asks.

"Nowhere. Just walking around."

"I'll walk around with you."

We head into the park and start along the path around Lost Lagoon. "One more week of torture," says Jason. "It's pointless even going to school right now. You gonna be around this summer?"

"Yeah. Should be." Not the time to tell him the Aspen Lake story. Not until I figure it out. "You?"

"Yup. I'll be hanging out at the beach or the skateboard park. And I might help our neighbor. He's doing some renos in his apartment and said he'll pay me eighteen bucks an hour."

"That's not bad."

"New iPhone! Come to me, baby!" He soccer dribbles a rock along the path, then kicks it into the lagoon. "What about you?"

"Beach."

"Nice."

We stop at a marshy spot and watch ducks swimming around in the reeds and bobbing their heads underwater.

"My Nana comes here every day and feeds them bread," says Jason. "It's like they know her now. It's crazy." He points. "See that big duck over there with the green head? That's Donald. And his little brown wife is Daisy."

I laugh.

"We're still working on the other names."

"Your Nana sounds nice," I say.

"Yup, she is."

All I know about my grandmother is she wants to be called Margaret. A tiny pause, then Jason says, "I'm living with her now."

"I live with my uncle and his wife," I say.

"And your little sister?"

"Yeah. Jane."

"She's cute."

That's it. End of questions. Jason's perfect for me.

By the time we've circled back to the seawall, the sun has almost disappeared and the freighters have turned on their night lights. Jason's told me all the features on the new iPhone and we've discussed all the best series on Netflix.

I'd like to wander around all night just talking. But it's a school night and Uncle Rob freaks if I'm late.

"I better go."

Jason flicks his hair back. "Curfew?"

"Yeah."

"That sucks. See you around?"

I sure hope so.

"See you," I say.

A huge crow stares down at me from the branches of a tree on Haro Street. I read online that people in the West End carry umbrellas because the crows are getting so aggressive and dive-bomb them. I think it's because someone fed them too many peanuts. Or something like that.

This crow looks sleepy. I run anyway. Not because of the crow. Not because I'm twenty minutes past my curfew.

Because I want to.

CHAPTER FOUR

"I knew you'd come around," says Uncle Rob.

He thinks I caved. Not true. It's just that Jane wants to go to Aspen Lake so badly ("Please, please, please, Rachel!") and I'm sick of the way Aleksandra treats her, like she's an annoying mosquito to bat away. I've come up with a plan. You have to take a bus to get there, so I'll go with Jane and stay just long enough to make sure she's safe. Then I'll zip back to Vancouver and Second Beach and Jason.

There's one blip in the plan—that's the part when I picture myself actually saying good-bye to Jane. We've never been apart. But I can't look after her for the rest of my life, either.

"What?" says Jason. "You're going, like, eight hours on a bus?"

This is our third time at the beach. He says he hasn't ditched the others, he's just taking a break. I'm stretched out on a towel, face down. He's making little piles of burning sand on my bare back. I've smeared on sunscreen and the sand is going to stick, but it feels incredible.

"So where is this place?" he says.

"I don't know exactly," I mumble into my towel. "The nearest town is called One Hundred Mile House. That's where the bus goes."

"One Hundred Mile House? That's the name of a town?"

"I know. It's weird."

"It's insane."

I stand up, brushing off loose sand. I'm suddenly feeling seriously queasy. Major mistake eating that chili dog that Jason insisted on buying. I never eat meat you can't identify. "Let's walk," I say.

I love English Bay. There are people everywhere; at tables outside restaurants, jogging, eating ice cream, holding hands. We stop at the A-maze-ing Laughter sculptures at the corner of Denman and Davie. It's one of Jane's favorite places. It's this group of huge bronze men in different positions, laughing like they're all in on some secret joke. It makes you smile just to look at them. Usually tourists are taking selfies, but right now it's quiet.

"I call these guys Mr. Happy," says Jason.

"They've all got the same name?"

"Yup. They're brothers."

I touch the smooth arm of the Mr. Happy in front of me. His mouth is stretched wide in a grin, his eyes all squinty.

"Let's go," says Jason.

We're planning on playing mini golf.

"One sec."

"Hey, Mr. Happy," I whisper. "What's your carapace?"

~

Jane's at the dentist so I head to the library on my own. I'm going to have to carry the books in my backpack on the bus so I'm rationing myself to three. *The Shadow Queen* by CJ Redwine. *The Shadow Soul* by Kaitlyn Davis. *Shadowshaper* by Daniel José Older.

I can read them in under a week, but I've got two weeks before they're overdue. I'll be back by then. On my way to the checkout desk, I pass the two little rooms with tables and chairs where you can shut the door and read or study with no one bugging you. It's not completely private because there's glass along the front. The first room's empty, but a guy with dark hair is hunched over the table in the second room, reading.

I open the door and plunk down in the chair opposite him. "Hi, Jason."

"Hey, Rach."

There's a stack of books on the table. Jason's been taking notes on a pad of yellow paper but he puts his pen down.

"Keep working," I say.

I pick up each book and examine the title. *The Night Sky, The Mystery of the Universe, Planisphere. Nightwatch.* The book in front of Jason is open to a double-spread of star charts. He scribbles a few more notes, then tips his chair back and says, "I'm done."

"So why do you do it?" I say.

"I dunno. I like knowing stuff about space."

"I mean, why do you sit at the back of the class with all the stupid kids?"

He flushes.

I could kick myself.

"That was a shitty thing to say," he says.

"Sorry."

He shrugs. "Coming to a new school at the end of the year, it was easier to sit at the back and be invisible. And Caitlin and those guys, they're friendly. They're okay. I like them."

Like I should talk. At least he's made friends.

"Let's go get something to eat," he says.

He puts *Planisphere* in his backpack and leaves the others in a neat stack on the table.

You never see stars like that in Vancouver.

"You realize that all these pictures are photoshopped," I say.

CHAPTER FIVE

Uncle Rob and Aleksandra are arguing about the bus. We've just finished a platter of sushi on the balcony overlooking Stanley Park. They're still out there with their coffee, and Jane and I are inside reading. Jane's lying on her back in the middle of the living room floor, holding her book over her face. I've positioned myself in a chair near the balcony door so I can keep track of their plans.

"I've got six interviews next week because we're hiring all new staff," says Uncle Rob. "I want to wait until I can drive them up to Aspen Lake myself."

Uncle Rob was managing the Sheridan Hotel in Warsaw in Poland. That's where he met Aleksandra. He transferred to the Sheridan in Vancouver and lately he's been super busy.

"You've taken too much time off already running back and forth to Aspen Lake," says Aleksandra. "For God's sake, your mother's going to meet them. Rachel's fifteen and Jane's not a baby." She's ticking off her points in her head. "They can sit near the driver, and they don't even need to get off the bus when it makes a stop. I'll pack them a lunch."

"It takes eight hours," says Uncle Rob. "They'll want to get off. I'm not comfortable with that. A lot of sketchy people hang around bus depots."

"We'll tell Rachel not to take her eyes off Jane for even a second."

"I should be there when they meet Dad," persists Uncle Rob. "With everything's that happened…I should never have stayed in Poland so long."

"Now you're blaming me?" says Aleksandra.

"Of course not. But every time I go to Aspen Lake, I get more worried."

"Your father just lost his son in August. He lost Layla years ago, and he's not well. What do you expect? Don't do this to me, Rob."

I've been collecting information about our instant family since December. This is what I have so far: Jane and I have grandparents (Margaret and Wayne Bird) who, it turns out, are not dead. They're alive and well and living on a ranch in Aspen Lake. My mother had a brother, Rob, who is also not dead. He's been living in Poland for the past eighteen years, but he came back to Vancouver to rescue me and Jane. My mother had another brother, Jimmy, who *is* dead.

All I know about him is that he had an accident with his hunting rifle. I don't need the details.

Aleksandra and Uncle Rob switch to Polish, which is

extremely annoying. I turn back to my book, but I make a mental note to tell Uncle Rob to drop it. Does he seriously think I need a babysitter?

And as for Jane, except for that *one time*, haven't I kept her safe her whole life?

~

The night before we leave, Jason and I walk along the seawall as far as Siwash Rock holding hands. I drag him over to one of Jane's memorial benches.

I read the saying on the back of the bench out loud. "*You cannot leave a place you've never been to.*"

"O-kay," says Jason.

"I haven't been able to figure this one out," I say. "The significance, I mean."

"Me neither," says Jason.

I laugh. "Yeah, right. Like you've tried."

"Hey, that hurts." Jason sits on the bench and pulls me down beside him. We compare legs. His are brown, mine are white. His are hairy, mine have little red dots on them from shaving too fast.

"Rachel?"

I'm ready. Our first kiss is over fast, but I like it, even though the whole time I'm praying I'm not blushing.

"I figured out what that saying means," he says. "It means you shouldn't go away to wherever it is that you're going."

Jason thinks my plan to come back to Vancouver has some holes. I've agreed that I need to work on it more.

"But I'm coming back for sure," I say.

I still haven't asked him why he lives with his grandmother. Or why he wants to be invisible. He's never asked what happened to Jane's arm. He's never asked what happened to our mother.

It's so much better that way.

CHAPTER SIX

As the bus winds its way up the Fraser Canyon, Jane's glued to the window. I can't look. This highway is seriously scary. There's a sheer drop off to the river on one side and a wall of rock on the other. I hope this bus driver is over-qualified and has at least twenty years of experience.

We're careening around corners and Bam! It's pitch black. Then back into daylight.

"What was that?" says Jane.

I crane my neck backwards. "A tunnel."

Each time we enter another tunnel, it's like we're belting straight into the side of the mountain. Jane adores it. When the highway finally straightens out, she announces, "That's seven tunnels."

"Well done." The woman across the aisle beams at her. "Very good counting."

Jane can probably count to infinity, but I don't point this out.

The woman's name is Doris. She's wearing a blue tracksuit and orange sneakers. She introduced herself when she got on the bus, struggling with a big basket and three shopping bags, at a town called Hope.

Hope! That's really what it's called. When I come back in my next life, I'm going to live in a place called Hope.

Doris reaches over now with an open bag of Licorice Allsorts. "No, thanks," I say, but Jane hunts around for the little round pink ones.

"You girls are adventurous to be traveling by yourselves," says Doris.

"We're going to stay with our grandparents," says Jane. "Our grandmother is Margaret and our grandfather is Wayne."

"Well, that sounds nice," says Doris.

"We saw Margaret once, but we've never even seen Wayne."

Doris sits up straighter. "Now that's interesting. Why—?"

"We didn't even *know* about Margaret and Wayne before."

"Well now, what do—?"

"And," Jane finishes, "Rachel has a boyfriend."

Jane's out of control.

I pull a word search book and a pen out of our backpack and shove them in front of her. She gets busy right away circling the capital cities of the world. Doris sighs and pulls out some knitting that just might be a purple sock.

We're passing miles and miles of forest with scattered houses and buildings and swampy looking ponds. Shit. Can I really leave Jane here?

My eyes keep shutting, and I let myself drift.

I wake up with a crick in my neck and gritty eyes. I check my watch. Less than an hour left. Both Jane and Doris are asleep now. Jane's crooked and her face is mushed against the window. I fold up my sweatshirt and slide it under her shoulder to prop her up.

I think about Jason. Is he my friend or is he my boyfriend? Do I want him to be my boyfriend? I sigh. This is too hard.

So, I think about what I saw last night. I got up at midnight to get a banana (the magnesium in bananas makes you sleepy, if you believe GoToSleep.com) and I ate it at the table where I'd left my laptop. I went back to my room to get the sunglasses Aura gave me (who knew there was an evil thing called blue light?), then googled Celtic knots for my future tattoo, found some images that looked interesting, and pressed *print*.

The printer, on a desk in the corner of the living room, banged and thumped. I remembered Aleksandra swearing after dinner because it had jammed up again. I was frantically trying to figure out how to hit *cancel* before I woke everyone up when there was a final choking gasp. I grabbed the edge of a creased paper and yanked it out, smoothing it flat. It was a letter written in Polish.

The heading at the top said,

WARSZAWA SZPITAL

Warszawa equals Warsaw. Not hard to figure that out. Szpital…. Hospital?

I dropped the paper on the floor, face down. But it's still bugging me.

Maybe it's a job offer for Aleksandra and she's going back to Warsaw. Maybe Uncle Rob doesn't know. Maybe Uncle Rob does know and he's going back to Warsaw, too.

Maybe Jane and I are going to Warsaw.

The bus driver shouts, "One Hundred Mile House. Five minutes."

I nudge Jane awake and start stuffing things in our backpack; Jane's empty juice boxes, her coloring book, her Go Fish card game, my water bottle. Jane slithers onto the floor and gathers up the crayons that have rolled under the seat.

I'd feel way better if we were getting off at Hope. This town is one hundred miles from somewhere.

Or nowhere.

CHAPTER SEVEN

I'm looking for the Margaret who stayed in a hotel in Vancouver for three days, wore the same black dress every day, and sat by herself on the balcony in the freezing cold, staring out at the park. I don't spot her anywhere among the people milling around the bus depot. But Jane does. She weaves through a bunch of kids and rushes up to a tanned woman in jeans and a red plaid shirt, who bends down and hugs her.

"You made it!" Margaret straightens and smiles at me. "Hi, Rachel."

"Hi."

The bus driver opens a hatch at the side of the bus and pulls out suitcases and boxes. I grab my duffel bag and Margaret takes Jane's and we haul them over to a black pickup truck. On the side, in gold letters, it says *Double D Ranch Aspen Lake* and underneath, a phone number. I heave our duffels into the open back, beside bags spilling over with groceries.

Jane claims the front seat, which is fine with me. There are more groceries on the backseat, but I push them over and create some space by the window.

"You two must be exhausted," says Margaret.

Just as she starts the truck, someone bangs on her window. She unrolls it and a man with a huge white moustache practically sticks his head inside.

"Oh my God, it is you. Margaret Bird. I was just meeting the bus to pick up a parcel and I saw your truck and I thought, oh my God, that's the Birds' truck. It's been a long time. Howard Wilson."

"Hello, Howard," says Margaret.

"So how long has it been? Eighteen years? We moved down to the coast but our son's still here. Sam. We're up here visiting for a few weeks. You remember our little Sam? You blink and suddenly he's forty!"

"That does happen," says Margaret. The truck's still running.

"Karen ran into Ann Frazier the other day. She said Rob's been living in Poland. And Jimmy—" For a millisecond, he loses steam. "We're real sorry about Jimmy, Margaret."

No comment from Margaret.

"And Layla. I always had a soft spot for Layla. She was a darling little girl. What's she up to?"

Ann Frazier, whoever she is, doesn't know. Now I'm on Margaret's side. Shut up, Howard.

He changes tactics. "You've got yourself some girls, I see. Hey, kids."

"Hey," says Jane.

"Where have you guys come from?"

"Vancouver," says Jane. "We went through seven tunnels and one of them was called Hell's Gate."

"Cool," says Howard.

"Margaret is our grandmother," Jane adds.

"Oh!" says Howard. "Well, how about that. Grand-daughters. Rob's kids?"

"No," says Margaret.

Howard waits, then tugs his moustache. "I'll get Karen to give you a call. Sam's set up a trampoline and one of those above-ground pools. Lindsay's bringing her gang down from Prince George. You remember—?"

"Yes, I remember Lindsay," says Margaret.

"Bring the girls over. We'll barbecue. And bring that old man of yours. I'd love to chew the fat with him."

Margaret moves the gear shift into drive. "We'll see. Good-bye, Howard."

She looks both ways and pulls out of the parking lot onto the highway.

"Can we go to their place?" says Jane. "Please, please, please? I've never been on a trampoline before."

Hanging out with a gang from Prince George? A *gang*?

"No," says Margaret. "We can't."

CHAPTER EIGHT

The bus depot is near the end of the town.

"Oh my God!" shouts Jane. "There's Burger King and Dairy Queen!" She practically spins right around backwards in the seat. "Can I get a cotton candy Blizzard? Please, please, please?"

While we're waiting at the drive-in window, I spot a pizza place, a fish and chips place, and lots of gas stations.

"That was it?" I say as we drive out of town.

"No," says Margaret. "There's lots more. There's all of Birch Avenue, which is really pretty and full of interesting stores. We'll explore it another day."

We drive for almost an hour along a two-lane highway. Margaret asks us about the bus ride, and she points out a few things along the way—"That's Bear Paw Resort. They have a small Farmer's Market on Saturdays…. That's the rodeo grounds…there's the public campground."

Mostly, we're quiet. The sun was shining when we left the bus depot, but now we're heading toward a band of dark clouds. I roll down my window and cool air blows on my face.

Margaret slows the truck and puts on her turn signal. She pulls into a gravel parking lot in front of a big green building. "I want to show you girls something."

We climb out of the truck. There are double doors in front of the building and a large wooden sign above them. Black letters on white. Margaret reads it out loud. "*The Daryl Bird Community Hall*. Daryl Bird was your great-great-grandfather."

Jane frowns. She's trying to figure this out. I don't know what to think. It's not normal to see your name on a building.

"Our family's been in Aspen Lake a very, very long time," says Margaret. "Daryl Bird came here on horseback over a hundred years ago and built our ranch. He married Daphne Bird, your great-great-grandmother. Do you remember the name of our ranch, Jane?"

"Double D," says Jane.

"That's right. Daryl and Daphne. That's where the Ds come from. They were pioneers."

"Wow," says Jane.

"Daphne?" I say.

Margaret smiles at me. "Your middle name. And Jane, your middle name is Mary. You're named after your great-grandmother, Mary Bird."

"Why?" says Jane.

"Well, your mother chose those names because they're special."

Daphne. I've always hated it. Who names their kid Daphne these days? It's so old-fashioned. Now I know why. I'm named after someone who was born more than a century ago.

"There's lots of things around here named after the Birds," says Margaret. "A road, a creek, a valley."

I'm slightly impressed.

~

"We're close now," says Margaret.

She turns off the highway onto a road on the right and we bump over a metal grill that makes the truck shake.

"What's that for?" says Jane.

"It's a cattle guard. Cows won't walk through it in case their feet fall through the spaces. It keeps them from roaming onto the highway."

The road is gravel. Clouds of dust billow around the truck, and I roll up the window. We bounce over ruts and holes, past some big fields, a pond. Most of the time we're in the forest. The trees aren't nearly as big as the trees in Stanley Park and a lot of them look dead.

"Pine beetle killed them," says Margaret. "It swept right through Aspen Lake."

We pass an open area with black stumps poking through long grass and carpets of blue flowers. It's beautiful, but Margaret mutters, "Clear-cut. You'd think the logging companies would have found a better way by now."

We go around another bend and cows are everywhere, milling all over the road. Margaret jams on the brakes.

These are seriously *big* black and brown cows with bony hips that jut out. They stare at us with sad eyes. Lots of tiny calves are scampering around. They're all bellowing. None of them are in a hurry to get out of the way. A massive brown cow lifts her tail, and a stream of runny black poop pours out.

"Eeeew," shrieks Jane.

It's gross alright. The back legs and rear ends of the cows are smeared with poop and flies are crawling on their faces. Margaret taps the horn, and we edge forward.

"You're going to hit them!" yells Jane.

"They'll get out of the way," says Margaret.

They take their time. A black cow with a white face stands her ground to the very end, pressing her face against the window beside me. Then she ambles off, a big sack with nipples swaying under her belly.

"These cows come from the High Valley Ranch," says Margaret, as she navigates around the last cow patty, her name for the puddles of poop on the road, which makes Jane laugh. "That's the ranch just past ours. It's free-range around here and the cows can graze wherever they want to. If we don't want them on our land, it's our responsibility to fence them out."

We're right under the black clouds now and it looks like it's going to pour any minute. Margaret stops again, this time in front of a wooden sign hanging over a gate that says *Double D Ranch*.

"Front passenger opens the gate," she says.

"Me?" says Jane.

"You," says Margaret. "You have to slide back that pole.

Then you can open the gate and we'll go through, and you can close it."

Jane leaps out. She wiggles the pole up and down, back and forth, and keeps looking back at Margaret who doesn't get out to help. This could take several days. I wish it would because we're here now and this is real, and my stomach is churning.

Finally, Jane gets it and when she scrambles back into the truck, Margaret says, "Well done. Number one rule on a ranch. Never open a closed gate and leave it open."

Number one obviously means there's a list of rules. The road is narrower now and climbs through leafy trees with pale gray trunks, and beside a twisty fence made of more poles.

"That's called a snake fence," says Margaret.

"A snake fence," repeats Jane. She's soaking in all these new words.

Then the trees end and green fields spread out on both sides.

Margaret points to a strip of slate gray water not that far away at the bottom of a sloping field. "That's Aspen Lake. Our ranch is at one end of it. You can walk across the field to get to the lake but it's easier if you take the trail. It's just through those trees along the side. The lake's weedy near the shore but there's a little beach and everyone used to love to swim there."

The road ends at a huge log house with a green metal roof.

Mom never told us she lived in a log house. Jane would have loved to know that. I would have loved to know that.

Margaret parks in front of a barn with a bleached white skull (cow or human?) hanging above the door. We could be in a movie about Alaska.

We sit here for a few seconds, and you can hear a ticking noise from the front of the truck. I take a big breath and clamber out first. Straight out of nowhere, a huge hairy beast barrels into me.

"Whoa!" I yell.

It's a dog with golden fur and floppy ears and it's barking like crazy. I shove it away while my brain registers *Uh-oh! Major Problem Ahead!*

Margaret leaps out of the truck. "DOWN, Bella! COME HERE! I'm so sorry, Rachel. Bella, that's very naughty!"

Margaret tells Bella to "SIT," and then says, "come on out, Jane. Bella just wants to say hello."

Then she peers up at the sky. "I felt a raindrop. Let's get those groceries and your bags inside before everything gets soaked. And then we'll phone Uncle Rob and let him know you're here."

Jane's staring at us through the window, her eyes like saucers. Margaret opens the passenger door.

Jane screams.

CHAPTER NINE

It's chaos.

I slam the truck door shut. Margaret grabs Bella's collar. The clouds open and buckets of rain pour down on us. In two seconds, I'm drowning.

"I'll put Bella inside," gasps Margaret.

The rain's bouncing off the truck like bullets. It's deafening.

Cripes. It's not rain now. It's pellets of hail and they hurt. They're like freaking golf balls! Hail in the summer? What *is* this place?

Jane opens the door a crack. "Is it snowing?" she says.

"Hailing. Get out. Run!"

~

Bella's locked in the laundry room, wherever that is (this is the first house I've been in that has a room just for laundry), and Jane and I are in the living room.

We changed into dry clothes in what Margaret calls "the boys' room." It's upstairs. We're getting the full tour of the house later. The boys' room is pretty bare: a bunk bed, a dresser, nothing on the walls.

"I've been using it for storage," Margaret explained when she took us up there. "But I cleaned everything out and I thought that both of you could start in here together. Once Jane settles in, I was thinking, Rachel, you might want to sleep—"

"We always share a room. I'll stay here."

I knew exactly what she was thinking. Upstairs in this house there's the boys' room, Margaret and Wayne's room, a bathroom, and a closed door at the end of the hallway. It has to be Mom's old room.

I'm not going in there.

Now Jane's curled up in a squishy, striped armchair beside a fireplace made of smooth round stones. I'm standing by the windows that go along one whole wall. The hail's turned back to sheets of rain and I can't see much.

To get into this house, you go through something called a mudroom, full of boots, shoes, jackets, and dog leashes hanging on hooks, then into the kitchen which has a big black wood-stove and a long wooden table. That's where Margaret is now, on the phone. I can hear her through the open door.

"You should have told me," she says. "What were you thinking, not to tell me?"

Long pause.

"She's been living with you since Christmas."

Long pause.

"What? There are no dogs in Vancouver?"

Margaret calls out. "Rachel, do you want to talk to Uncle Rob?"

"No," I call back.

"Okay then," says Margaret. "I don't know.... No, I can tell them. I just think I should wait until they're settled in."

She shuts the door. Whatever she's planning to tell us, it doesn't sound like anything I want to know. I'll be long gone by then.

PLAN A: GOOGLE THE BUS SCHEDULE AND FIGURE OUT HOW TO GET TO ONE HUNDRED MILE HOUSE.

I refuse to feel guilty about Jane.

~

"Could you please give me the Wi-Fi password after dinner?" I say, very politely.

I'm pouring glasses of milk, Jane's setting the table. Margaret gave her three of everything, placemats, napkins, knives, and forks. Wayne's not eating with us. I don't know why, and I don't know where he is but I'm not asking.

"Pardon me?" says Margaret.

"The Internet password."

She's forgotten it. Uncle Rob will know, so I may have to break down and talk to him. I'm not happy with him at the moment because I'm holding him and Aleksandra totally responsible for all this.

And then a little trickle of fear curls in my stomach.

"I've never bothered to hook up," says Margaret. "I'd need to get a satellite dish or something. The Aspen Lake School is open on Tuesday and Friday afternoons in the summer, and you could go up there if you like. There are also public computers in the library in town. I could drop you off on my shopping day."

"Don't you ever use Google? Don't you have email? Don't you pay bills online?"

"No, I don't."

I can pass on things like Facebook and Snapchat, but I *have* to be able to google stuff, and not just on Tuesdays and Fridays.

"Please tell me you have cell service," I say.

"I only get one bar of cell reception. On a very good day. Most days no bars. That's according to your Uncle Rob. I wouldn't know because I don't use it."

One bar? *No* bars? I've never even heard of that. "How am I going to use my phone?"

"I don't know. Jane, could you look in the fridge for the ketchup?"

How am I going to text Jason?

Margaret lifts a casserole dish out of the oven and sets it on the counter. "Jane, you sit down. I'll dish this up and, Rachel, you can carry the plates to the table."

Margaret scoops out spoonfuls of something that's lumpy

and has peas in it. Millions of peas. My heart plummets because Jane doesn't—

"What is this?" Jane's staring at her plate.

"Tuna fish casserole," says Margaret.

"I don't eat peas," says Jane.

Margaret picks up her fork. "Then you'll have to eat around them."

"And I despise tuna fish."

"No, you don't," I say.

"Yes, I do." Jane's face darkens. "Uncle Rob lets me have frosted cornflakes for dinner."

"He does not," I say.

"Yes," says Jane.

"No."

Jane kicks the table leg. Her glass of milk tips over and milk floods her plate and streams across the table. My mouth is full of casserole but now it's stuck in my throat.

A crappy memory rushes back—the time when Aleksandra brought chicken curry home from the deli and told Jane she had to eat it. Jane threw her glass of milk at Aleksandra and Aleksandra went ballistic. Jane kicked the wall all the way to her bedroom. *Why couldn't she just eat the bread, Aleks?* Uncle Rob had said. *Why did you have to ruin our dinner?*

I'm watching Margaret's face. She stands up and takes Jane's plate. "I'll make you some oatmeal while you clean up this milk. No frosted cornflakes. And then I'm going to get a tray ready for your grandfather."

"*Thank* you," says Jane. "With brown sugar, please, please, please."

In a few minutes, the milk is mopped up and oatmeal's burbling in a pot on top of the woodstove.

"Hey," says Jane. "Can you play games on the computers at that school?"

"I think so," says Margaret. "And Rachel? I *have* heard that there's better cell reception in the middle of the lake."

A feeble ray of hope. "Do you have a boat?"

CHAPTER TEN

"What about our teeth?" says Jane.

"We'll skip that tonight." Margaret sounds dead tired.

I crouch on the floor and root around in Jane's duffel bag. She needs to get to bed. I pull out a stack of T-shirts. Shit. Where's Hoodie?

"Where's Hoodie?" says Jane.

"Um."

Don't panic.

Hoodie was Mom's. It's red with a fleecy white lining. For the first two months, after we moved in with Uncle Rob and Aleksandra, Jane lived inside Hoodie. It hangs down to her knees and the arms are so long, she looks like a chimpanzee. She wouldn't let Aleksandra wash it because she said it would make Mom's smell go away. Uncle Rob used to make jokes. *I see a nose. She's in there, somewhere.* Now Jane just sleeps in it.

"Aha!" I pull Hoodie out of the bag. There's something else lying flat at the very bottom. A folded plastic mattress cover. This might be the only useful thing Aleksandra's ever done for me. I glance at Margaret, who's pulling down the blind. Jane made me swear not to tell her, so I pile Jane's T-shirts and shorts on top of it.

Jane strips down to her underpants. There's one tense moment when Margaret sees the tight puckered skin that runs from Jane's shoulder to her elbow on her right arm. I bite my lip. Margaret doesn't say anything, and then Jane's inside Hoodie.

"Bottom or top bunk?" I say.

"I don't know."

She's pooped. "Bottom then. Crawl in."

I'm rummaging around in my duffel now, hunting for my brand-new kindle that Uncle Rob gave me last night. We loaded it with the *His Dark Materials* trilogy by Philip Pullman, which Uncle Rob let me buy even though I've read it before. I'm not planning on trying to go to sleep for hours but I'm already dreading it.

Margaret's smiling at Jane. "She's out like a light. I usually make myself some cocoa at night. Would you like some?"

"No. Thank you. I'm just going to read in here."

Aura says that's a terrible habit of mine. Saying no automatically before stopping to think what I really want. And what I really want right now is some cocoa but it's too late. Margaret says, "Goodnight, Rachel," and she's gone.

I find the kindle and change into my long night shirt that's covered in dogs wearing pajamas and the words "Ruff

Night." I climb up the ladder to the top bunk. I play around with the buttons on my kindle, checking out *library* and *home* and *settings*.

Right. No Internet.

Downstairs, Bella's barking. I tap on *The Golden Compass* and try to read but I can't concentrate. Margaret said they used to keep a canoe at the beach by the lake. She hasn't been down there for years, but she figures it's still there. If I can find it tomorrow, I'll paddle it to the middle of the lake and text Jason. Two words. *Save me!*

Somewhere down the hall a phone is ringing. At least twenty times. Then it stops. It doesn't ring again. I'm betting Margaret doesn't have anything as modern as call display. So why didn't she answer it?

~

2 A.M.

I pick up my kindle, swing my legs over the side of the bunk bed, and drop softly to the floor. I don't need Jane awake, too.

I can navigate Uncle Rob's apartment in the dark like a cat. But this is new territory. I tiptoe down the hall, past an open bedroom door. A lamp on a small table in the room is turned on and there's a jumble of blankets on the bed, but no Margaret or Wayne. I'm starting to think that this might be just Margaret's room. So where's Wayne in this great big house? Maybe this is like *Jane Eyre* where Mr. Rochester locks his insane wife on the third floor of Thornfield Hall because she's so violent. But in this case it's Wayne who's locked up.

I adjust my plan. Jane's going to have to come back to Vancouver with me.

I pause at the bottom of the stairs. Music drifts from the living room. I peek inside. Margaret's sitting in an armchair, eyes closed. Bella's lying half in and half out of a round dog bed. She sees me and thumps her tail on the floor.

Margaret opens her eyes. "Ah," she says. "A fellow night wanderer. I hope my music's not too loud."

"No, it's okay."

Night wanderer. I like that.

"There's a pot of tea in the kitchen," says Margaret. "I switch from cocoa to chamomile tea after midnight. But there's still some cocoa in a pot on the stove if you'd rather. Then come and join me."

"No…. Um, yes. Thank you."

The pot's on the woodstove and the cocoa's still warm. I pour myself a mug. I bring it to the living room and sit down on one end of a flowered couch. Bella jumps up, pads over, and tries to scramble into my lap.

"She's only allowed on that old purple couch," says Margaret.

I move to the purple couch and set my mug on the floor, away from Bella's wagging tail. She springs up beside me and licks my hand.

"And she's supposed to stay on that blanket."

Bella scoots around in circles and scrunches an old plaid blanket into a ball. Now she's one hundred percent off the blanket and on top of me.

Margaret sips her tea. "Tell me why Jane is so frightened of dogs."

"Our neighbor's dog bit her," I say. "When she was three. On her nose."

"Oh no."

"It wasn't that bad a bite."

There's a tiny white scar on the tip of Jane's nose but it only shows up when she cries.

"But pretty scary for a little girl," says Margaret.

"Yeah. This, well, our other neighbor called the cops and she told them it was a pit bull, but it wasn't. She told the cops that they had to do something. She kept going on and on and Jane was listening and then she freaked out. She wasn't even crying that hard until then."

"That's unfortunate," says Margaret.

I pick up my mug of cocoa.

Margaret sighs. "I wish I'd known that before. But I know now. I'll have to figure out what to do."

But she doesn't really know. She doesn't know that it was Mom who called the cops. Mom who screamed at them and said the dog had to be destroyed.

"What did the police do?"

"Nothing. We moved."

Again.

My hands are sweaty. I put my mug down before it slips right out of my hand. I don't talk about any of the bad stuff except to Aura. That's *my* rule. I don't know what just happened. But from now on, I'll keep my mouth shut.

Margaret's eyes close. I stroke Bella's soft ears for a long time. Then I open my kindle.

A night wanderer. That's me.

CHAPTER ELEVEN

In the morning, I hang my head over the bunk. Jane's gone. I jump down and check her bed. The sheets and plastic mattress cover that I slid underneath her are wet. I roll the sheets into a ball and leave them on the floor until I can find a garbage bag. I think I can air dry the mattress cover.

Air dry the mattress cover, find a garbage bag, hide the wet sheets, find dry sheets, find the washing machine and dryer, and figure out how to wash the sheets without Margaret knowing. Complicated! I get dressed and make my way to the kitchen. There's a carton of orange juice, a plate of pancakes covered with a tea towel, and a bottle of maple syrup on the counter. There's also a tray with an eggshell in a cup, an empty mug, and a plate with crusts of toast. Wayne's breakfast, I bet. But where's Wayne? This is starting to get spooky.

Come to think of it, where's Bella?

The window over the kitchen sink looks out to the front of the house where the pickup's parked. Beside the barn there's a long wooden shed, a log fence, and a flower bed filled with yellow daisies. I didn't notice any of that yesterday in the rain. I drink my orange juice, and then take my pancakes through the living room and outside to a wide verandah that goes all along the back of the house. Last night, everything was gray and dripping. But now the sky is dark blue, way bluer than in Vancouver and, in the distance, the lake is sparkling. Red roses climb all over a gray wooden fence that separates the field from a strip of grass.

Something catches my eye—a little house with glass walls tucked at the far end of the verandah. It's full of colors. Orange, purple, red, green, yellow. The sun's slanting through the glass, turning the colors into jewels. Birds? I set my plate down on a table and walk closer.

Butterflies. The little glass house is full of butterflies.

I open the small glass door and step into a cloud of butterflies, folded out of paper and hanging on threads. Some are bright solid colors and some have swirly designs on them. They have long pointed wings and wings that curve. They're all super delicate. Fragile. Really beautiful. Who made them?

I blow gently on a butterfly. It dances on its thread. A butterfly house. It's perfect. Then I find one, different from the others. Pure white. I move closer, butterflies brushing my cheeks. I touch a white wing. The butterfly sways back and forth.

A name is written on the wing.

Stephanie.

~

Margaret and Jane have come out to the verandah.

"We went to see the horses," says Jane. "There's a baby one for me."

"A pony, not a baby," says Margaret.

"Her name's Dixie," says Jane.

"We've only got the two geldings here now," says Margaret. "Magic and Dancer. I borrowed Dixie for the summer so we'll all have a horse to ride."

"What's a gelding?" says Jane.

"A castrated stallion," I say.

I've already decided to pass on horseback riding.

"Can we go riding now?" says Jane. "Please, please, please."

"No," says Margaret. "Right now, I need my second cup of coffee and then I'm gardening before it gets too hot."

She goes back inside, and I flop down on a fat pillow on a chair that's woven from sticks.

Jane's hopping up and down. "Margaret didn't see that I'm wearing flip-flops until we got out there. I could've got stepped on. You have to wear boots around horses. Margaret's going to find us some boots."

Horse rules.

"Nice," I say.

But I'm not thinking about horses. When Margaret comes back with her coffee, I say, pointing, "Those butterflies in that glass house? Who made them?"

"Your mother."

I didn't see that coming. I dig my fingernails into the palms of my hands and focus on the sharp stab.

"I want to see them, too," says Jane.

Margaret and I stand by the door of the glass house while Jane goes inside. I don't have to tell her to be careful. She's surrounded by butterflies and she's holding her breath. I don't know why but I'm hoping she doesn't spot the white butterfly, and she doesn't.

"It was originally a place for me to start seeds," says Margaret. "Like a mini greenhouse. We get so much sun out here. Then Wayne finally built me a proper greenhouse out behind the vegetable garden and Layla claimed it for her butterflies."

I nod. I want to listen, and, at the same time, I don't.

"It's called origami. Japanese paper folding. It takes a lot of patience. Your mom was an expert."

Mom was an expert? Mom, who started knitting a hat for Jane and then tossed it on the floor in the corner of her bedroom. Mom, who couldn't stay in the kitchen long enough to cook anything except Kraft dinner. Mom, who paced around, lighting cigarettes and stubbing them out a minute later.

Mom made the butterflies? I find that hard to believe.

CHAPTER TWELVE

Margaret takes Bella for a walk in the fields, and I stay with Jane in the house. Then it's back to the laundry room for Bella while Margaret gives us a tour of her vegetable garden. It's inside a tall weathered gray fence which keeps out deer, rabbits, gophers, and something called marmots. There are flowers and lots of green things growing.

Jane reads out loud all the labels on the little wooden sticks that mark each row. "*Baby carrots, golden beets, spinach, purple bush beans, swiss chard, ruta...ruta....*"

"Rutabaga," says Margaret. "They're like turnips."

Jane's forgotten that she hates all vegetables. Margaret shows her how to pull up a carrot. Presto! It's magic.

The mosquitoes in here are very annoying. Margaret's doing something called thinning the lettuce and Jane's pulling up hundreds of carrots and I'm ready to leave and go look for the canoe. It's so hot and I could use a swim. Then a car horn beeps.

Margaret looks up. "Now who can that be?"

She heads for the driveway and Jane and I trail after her. A silver car is parked behind the pickup truck. On the side of the car it says *Amber Gordon Vacation Land Realtors, 100 Mile House, BC.* A woman with short curly brown hair and freckles, wearing a jean skirt and a yellow blouse, hops out.

"Hi, Margaret," she says.

"Hello, Amber," says Margaret.

Amber stares at me and Jane. "Hey," she says.

"Hey," says Jane.

Margaret says, "This is Rachel, and this is Jane. Layla's girls."

"Welcome to Aspen Lake!" says Amber.

"What brings you here today?" says Margaret.

Amber pulls her eyes away from us. "Me and Cassie are going to stay at Mom and Dad's for a week. So, I thought I could pick up those maps we were talking about."

"I told you, Amber, I haven't made any firm decisions yet."

"I thought we'd agreed to list it."

"No, we didn't."

"Is that because of Wayne? Is he still—?"

"Amber," says Margaret.

That means *shut up, Amber.* Why? I'm starting to think there's something seriously wrong with my grandfather.

And listing? They're selling the ranch? Margaret made such a big deal about Daryl Bird building this ranch a million years ago. She didn't say a word about selling it. Not that I care.

"No worries," says Amber. "But *just in case*, I want to start to reorient myself, make sure I'm clear on the property lines. I mean, I remember it pretty well, but—"

"I'm sure you do."

"I'm thinking, *if* you decide to go ahead with this and *if* we move fast, we could be ready in September. We'll have offers pretty quick and then…." Amber chews her bottom lip.

Margaret presses her fingers against her forehead and closes her eyes.

"Oh my God, I'm so sorry," says Amber. "I don't want to trigger one of your migraines. That's absolutely the *last* thing I want to do. It's just—"

"Alright," says Margaret, "I'll get you the maps but it's going to take me a few minutes to find them. And it doesn't mean we've decided to sell."

"Great!" Amber glances at the house. "Christ, it's hot out here."

Five seconds of silence. Then Margaret says, "You'd better come in and wait in the kitchen."

~

Amber and I sit at the kitchen table drinking water from the jug in the fridge. Jane's disappeared with Margaret.

"You like it here?" says Amber. "So far?"

"Yup."

"I'm really sorry about your mom."

I pick up my glass and take it to the sink.

"I still can't believe it. God. Layla. I grew up on the High

Valley Ranch. That's the ranch next to this. My parents are Martin and Susan."

Right. The cows all over the road. I finish my water. What's keeping Margaret?

"I used to come over here all the time. Lots of good memories. I stayed around for a year after, well, after everything happened. Then I went to Kamloops. Got married. Divorced. Now I'm back in Hundred Mile in an apartment. Who'd have thought I'd end up there?"

I'm thinking that probably all the local people drop the One and House and just say Hundred Mile (and I do like to fit in) when Amber adds, "But at least I've got Cassie."

Am I supposed to know who Cassie is?

"Cassie's my daughter." She drums her fingers on the table. "How old is Jane?"

"Six."

"No way! Cassie's six too! Grade one in September, right?"

"Yup."

"That's gotta be karma or something. They can play together. Cassie will love that. And if you want, you and me could go riding sometime. I've got my horse at Mom and Dad's. I could show you Butterfly Lake. I've been trying to get my courage up to go back there. Layla named it that. It was one of our favorite places."

"I don't really ride," I say. "But thanks anyway."

"I guess you've seen the Butterfly House."

"Yes."

"Layla was totally into butterflies."

I'd gotten that.

"How long are you going to be here?"

"Don't know."

Margaret finally comes back. Jane's holding a fat cardboard tube that she bangs on the top of my head.

"Great! You found the maps." Amber grabs the tube out of Jane's hand. "I won't keep bugging you. But we don't want to wait till winter. It's too hard in the snow." She clasps her hand to her mouth. "Oops. I know. I meant, if you want to sell."

A door at the back of the kitchen flies open.

A tall, heavy man stands there, leaning on two canes. He's got long gray hair, swept back, and he's wearing jeans with a huge silver buckle in the middle of his belt.

"Hi there, Wayne," says Amber. "I just dropped by to—"

"How dare you come in this house with all your talk about selling!" he says. "Get out! Get out!"

He smashes the tube of maps out of Amber's hand with one of his canes.

Amber leaps back. "Hey! Careful!"

"I decide if this ranch is going to be sold. Not you and not Margaret."

"Nothing is—" says Margaret.

"I will never sell it!"

Jane bursts into tears.

"Wayne," says Margaret. "Please. The girls."

For the first time, Wayne looks right at me. "Jesus!"

I step back. What's wrong with him? What did I do?

CHAPTER THIRTEEN

Amber grabs the tube of maps. "I'm outta here!"

"I'll talk to you later, Amber," says Margaret.

Jane's still sobbing and Wayne's not doing anything. He's just standing there.

"Rachel, take Jane outside," says Margaret.

We take a detour upstairs and change into our bathing suits. The kitchen door is closed when we go past, but I can hear the murmur of Margaret's voice. Up and down. Calm.

~

PLAN B: ASK AMBER FOR A RIDE TO (ONE) HUNDRED MILE (HOUSE).

~

I'm floating on my back, staring up at one puffy white cloud in the blue sky. I just swam through clumps of brown weeds and long ropey things that wrapped around my legs. I'm keeping my feet up just to be safe.

Jane's playing at the side of the lake. Margaret calls it a beach but really, it's just an opening in the bushes. There's a grassy bank, big mossy rocks, and a half-submerged tree that fell down.

No canoe.

I tread water so I can check on Jane. She finally stopped talking about Wayne, who scared her half to death. She's wading up to her knees, poking around, and stirring up mud. I read *Wind in the Willows* to her a couple of months ago and she's pretending to look for Ratty and Mole and Toad Hall.

I catch a glimpse of something orange, a little ways along the shore. I swim over, and wade the last bit, the mud squishing between my toes. Lying upside down, half buried in long grass, is an orange canoe. The paint's peeling back in ragged curls. Jane notices and splashes over.

"Help me turn it over," I say.

We slide our fingers under one side, grab on tight and, grunting, flip the canoe. A huge, tangled ball of dried brown grass is stuck under the front seat.

"That's some kind of nest," I say. "Better not—"

Jane pounces on it. She pulls it out in clumps.

"Mice," I say, though I haven't got a clue. "They've all grown up and left home."

The canoe looks old, but I don't see any obvious holes.

"Can we go for a ride?" says Jane.

"We need paddles." I gaze around. "Help me look for them."

We hunt in the long grass, pull back branches, peer behind logs. I wipe the sweat trickling down my neck and bat away mosquitoes.

"Margaret will know," I say.

~

Margaret opens the door of an old shed by the barn. She flips on an overhead light bulb. I've never seen so much junk. A plaid couch with a ripped back, tires wrapped in plastic, a saddle, three wooden dressers, a toilet, a fridge, a crib, a wheelbarrow with no wheel. There are stacks of cardboard cartons, some labeled with black felt pen. CAMPING DISHES, NATIONAL GEOGRAPHICS, MUGS.

"I blame this on your grandfather," she says. "He's the most disorganized man in the world. And he won't give anything away."

"Paddles," Jane reminds her.

"They could be anywhere. I'll leave you girls to hunt, and good luck."

"We'll start at opposite ends," I say. "And work toward each other."

After twenty minutes, I'm baking hot and dusty. The swim seems forever ago.

I'm temporarily distracted from paddles when I find an old red bicycle leaning against the back wall. The tires are flat, and it only has three gears, but I like biking. It's Jane who finds the paddles, poking out from behind a mattress that's leaning against the wall beside a pile of lifejackets. She does a victory dance.

I ignore her. I've left the bike and I'm investigating a row of boxes in the corner of the shed. The flaps have popped open on a few of them. They're full of books.

Jane drops the paddles and plunks down on the floor beside me and we pull them out. We find lots of *Harry Potter*, all seven books from *The Chronicles of Narnia*, Susan Cooper's *The Dark is Rising* series, *Charlie and the Chocolate Factory*, *James and the Giant Peach*, and a stack of *Nate the Great* books.

"*Nate the Great!*" shrieks Jane. She spreads them out on the floor, checking to see if there are any she hasn't read yet.

I flip open the Narnia books and a few of the Harry Potters. A bookplate is glued to the inside cover of each book with a picture of a rabbit sitting on a stack of books. Underneath the rabbit are the words *This book belongs to* and then *Layla Bird* in that big loopy handwriting that I practiced so hard in grade three until I found out that nobody handwrites anymore.

I put them down. I'm ready to get out of here when I spot a book with a yellow paper butterfly on the cover. It looks just like the butterflies in the Butterfly House. The book is called *The World of Origami Butterflies*. No bookplate, just *Layla Bird* inside the cover. I sink back on my heels and flip through it slowly. Every page has a photograph of a different butterfly perched outside on a real flower or in a tree. Opposite the photographs are instructions and diagrams. Step by step. Dotted lines, creases, and folds.

"What's this for?" says Jane. She's left *Nate the Great* and she's holding up a small box. She opens it. "Paper."

"Let me see."

The box is full of paper squares, some solid colors, some patterned. It must be special origami paper to make the butterflies. Everything I need.

Mom did it.

How hard could it be?

~

Paddling a canoe is tricky. I think you're supposed to sit on the little seat in the back, but when I try that, the bow sticks way up in the air. Sitting in the bow doesn't work either, so I've settled for the seat in the middle. I keep switching sides with the paddle because if I don't, I spin in circles. I'm aiming for a little island in the middle of the lake, but it seems to be getting farther away, not closer.

I grip the sides of the canoe and slide carefully into the back again while it wobbles wildly from side to side. Three strokes on the left. Three strokes on the right. My shoulders are aching, so I rest the paddle and float. Strings of brown weeds are growing up from the bottom of the lake and schools of tiny silver fish dart by. Two dragonflies chase each other across the water.

Forget the island. This has got to be far enough. I dig my phone out of my pocket and hold it up.

No bars. *No freaking bars.*

PLAN C: FIND A BICYCLE PUMP. PUMP UP THE TIRES ON THE BIKE IN THE SHED AND RIDE (JANE CAN DOUBLE ON THE BACK) TO HUNDRED MILE.

~

After Jane's gone to bed, I'm at the kitchen table, working on the first butterfly in the book because it's probably the easiest.

I crumple up my fifth try. I'm totally wasting paper. I've restricted myself to the boring colours to practice on. Brown, gray, olive green. The box is full of gorgeous colors too: turquoise, silver, and gold, and papers with swirly patterns, polka dots, and even tiny flowers. But I need to get better at this first.

I choose dark plum for my last try. I've memorized the first steps by now. Dotted lines mean you're supposed to fold. Arrows tell you which way. This time I get to step five. I'm hopeful.

Rotate the paper ninety degrees clockwise. Turn the model over.

Got it.

Valley fold the bottom edge to the top.

What exactly is a valley fold? I guess.

Step seven: squash fold the left half.

Squash fold? Dotted lines and arrows everywhere now. I fold and crease and squash and turn.

Your butterfly should look like this.

Mine doesn't. Not even close.
It doesn't have wings.

~

4 A.M.

Bella's taken over the old purple couch. She's sprawled on her back, snoring. I'm curled up beside her, sipping Margaret's tea, which she buys at a health food store in Hundred Mile. Sleepytime. It's full of flowers.

"Wayne has rheumatoid arthritis," says Margaret. She's in the rocking chair by the stone fireplace with a pile of lime green knitting in her lap. A sweater for Jane. Jane adores lime green but if the wool is scratchy, she won't wear it.

"He hates people to see him like this."

"Is it painful?"

"Very. Sometimes unbearable when he has what the doctors call a flare. And then other times, not so bad. He must have seen Amber's car through his window. She's used to him but still, that was extremely unpleasant. And it was a terrible introduction for Jane."

"She's scared of him now," I say.

"I know. I'm very angry at Wayne for that. But it was hard for him today. With his arthritis and worrying about the ranch. He'll have a good day soon. And then he'll want to visit with you."

"So why *are* you selling the ranch?"

"*Thinking* of selling it," says Margaret. Her knitting slips to the floor but she just leaves it. "Wayne can't do the work anymore. Your Uncle Jimmy was pretty well running the ranch for years. And now, everything's falling apart. There are so many fences to repair and maintenance for the machinery. It never ends."

She picks up her teacup, sets it down again. "We've leased the hayfields to Amber's parents, Martin and Susan, and we sold our cows, but it's still more than we can manage. Your grandfather has trouble accepting that."

I rub one of Bella's ears gently between my fingers. It's like silk.

"He doesn't want me here," I say.

"Of course he does."

"Then why did he react like that when he saw me?"

"Well," says Margaret, "it's because you look exactly like your mother did when she was fifteen. I told him that when I came back from Vancouver in December. But I still don't think he was expecting that."

"He didn't like Mom?" I say.

"He adored her," says Margaret.

CHAPTER FOURTEEN

At breakfast, the phone rings once.

Margaret waits fifteen seconds.

It rings again.

She picks it up. "Hello, Rob."

"It's a secret code," I whisper to Jane, who's dipping her finger into a bowl of muffin batter.

"No, he's asleep," says Margaret. "He's lifting himself in and out of bed...there's no need for you to come up for a while...have a rest from all that driving...everyone's fine...yes, he's still managing the toilet on his own."

Too much information.

I take my plate of toast out to the verandah. No wind. Time to get back in the canoe.

~

It's sunny again. Hot. Margaret's anxious about forest fires. She said that the rain and hail on the night we came won't help. It's been dry for weeks. Most of the shore of Aspen Lake is forest except for three fields that come right to the water. Forest fires. My list of things to worry about just gets bigger and bigger.

I paddle until I can't see the house anymore. At this end of the lake, there's this ranch and the High Valley Ranch. The summer cottages and the houses where people live all year round are at the other end of the lake near the school and store.

The lake is like glass. This is the farthest away I've ever been in my life from other people. Even on the trails in Stanley Park, there's always someone right around the corner and you can hear cars in the distance. Here, I'm totally alone.

I'm getting the hang of paddling now. This time I get close to the island. I glide into a patch of lily pads that bump and rustle against the bottom of the canoe. A few more strokes and I'm stuck. It's a perfect place to check the signal.

Two bars. There are three texts from Aura.

A photo of her and Mike standing in front of the Eiffel Tower pops up.

Two days ago:

AURA: Went to the Louvre. Mona Lisa overrated. Venus de Milo very cool.

Today:

AURA: Where r u?????

How do I explain all this?

ME: One hundred miles from nowhere.

Technically, if you count the drive out to this ranch, it's probably more like one hundred and forty miles.

A black and white head pops out of the water, right between me and the island. It's a bird and it's so close I can see its red eye. It stares at me, and I stare back. Opening its bill it makes this long warbling sound. The noise is eerie but it's so beautiful. It cries again and the back of my neck prickles. I didn't know a bird could do that.

It dives. I scan the water and find it, quite far away, off the end of the island. I wait, hoping it will make its cry again, but it doesn't, and then it's gone. I let out my breath. That was amazing.

I check the bars on my phone. They've disappeared. This is ridiculous. I killed myself to get here and it gave me like ten seconds. Jason's going to wonder what's going on.

Wait. He didn't text *me*.

Oh God, I do not need this.

I paddle through the lily pads, out of the bright sunshine into the cool green shade beside the island. I search for a place to land. It's a jumble of bushes, fallen trees, and boulders and I'm wearing flip-flops.

Scrap that. I paddle back into the sun. Something in the distance catches my eye, partly hidden in trees, on the shore not far from where I found the canoe. It's big and white and I have no idea what it is.

I'm going to check it out.

~

I tie the yellow rope hanging from the bow of the canoe to a long branch jutting over the water. Pulling off my flip-flops, I climb out. I wade across slippery rocks, knee deep, and scramble onto a boulder. From there, I hop onto the ground.

A little ways back from the water there's some kind of gigantic tent made out of grayish white canvas. It's in a small clearing. Behind it, a path disappears into thick trees.

It has a high dome-like roof and one small window beside a wooden door. I peer through it, but the glass is dusty and streaked with dirt and I can't see inside.

I walk all around the tent, stepping carefully over sharp pinecones and little sticks and pebbles. No more windows.

It's so quiet. So still. Not even a breath of breeze. It feels abandoned, like whoever owns it doesn't come here anymore. I want to go inside but I can't.

There's a padlock on the door.

When I get back to the canoe, I look back. It feels like someone's watching me through that grimy window.

Creepy.

CHAPTER FIFTEEN

"Put one scoop of kibble in Bella's bowl," says Margaret.

Jane measures carefully. Margaret opens a can of dog food called Chicken and Vegetable Stew. It smells like people food. "Put a big spoonful of this on top," she tells Jane. "I'll go and get Bella. And I'll keep her on her leash."

She disappears down a hallway behind the kitchen. So that's where the laundry room is…with the washer and dryer! I've already found the garbage bags (on a shelf in the mudroom) and the dry sheets (a cupboard beside the upstairs bathroom). So far, I have one peed-on sheet in a garbage bag under the bunk bed.

We hear claws scrabbling on the floor and panting and Margaret shouting, "CALM DOWN, BELLA!"

Bella drags Margaret into the kitchen. Jane backs right up against the fridge. Bella's front feet splay sideways.

Food! Food! I smell food! Where's my food? Bring it on!

Did Margaret forget to feed this dog for a couple of days? For a month?

"She's more Wayne's dog than mine," she says. "She behaves much better with him."

Well, that's not saying much.

Bella wolfs down her kibble and chicken stew. Then she motors toward Jane, her tail waving a hundred miles an hour.

Margaret pulls back on the leash. "Would you like to try to pet her, Jane?" she says.

"No," says Jane.

"I'd put her in with Wayne but he's having one of his flare ups right now." Margaret's not giving up. "Let's let her stay with us for a while."

Jane shakes her head. "No."

Margaret sighs.

"Back to the laundry room, Bella, you ungrateful fiend!" I say. "Bread and water for you! Off with your head!"

Margaret drags a whining Bella out of the kitchen.

My little sister has no mercy.

～

Margaret's made spaghetti with Bolognese meat sauce for our dinner and a plate of scrambled eggs on a tray for Wayne.

"No sauce on Jane's!" I say. "Just butter—"

Too late.

Jane eyes her spaghetti. Her face is a thundercloud. She turns the bowl upside down.

Bad move.

After Jane cleans up Bolognese sauce and noodles, Margaret makes her a bowl of oatmeal with brown sugar.

Round two. Who won? I don't know. I must look worried because Margaret says, "She won't starve."

"Yeah, but what about the Canadian Food guide? The four food groups? She's going to get scurvy."

"What's scurvy?" says Jane.

"Your tongue turns black, and all your teeth fall out, and your eyeballs roll backwards, and you go insane from lack of vitamin C."

"Liar," says Jane.

My little sister gets smarter every day.

~

2 A.M.

"It's called a yurt," says Margaret. "They're used by nomads in places like Turkey and Mongolia. Only, those ones are made out of animal skins."

"I thought it was some kind of giant tent," I say.

"Well, it's like a tent."

Margaret's knitting the green sweater for Jane. I'm stretched out on the floor beside Bella, reading *The Subtle Knife* on my kindle. I scratch behind her ears.

In my next life, I'm going to come back as Bella.

"The nomads take them down and carry them with them when they move around," says Margaret.

"Where did the yurt come from?"

"Your Uncle Jimmy built it. He had help but it was his idea. He researched it and ordered the materials. He was brilliant at that sort of thing."

"Did he live in it?"

"For many years."

"In the winter too?"

"Yes, even when it got really cold. He had a little generator for power, and he could run a heater and some lights. He loved the yurt."

Margaret stops knitting.

"I'd like to go inside, but the door's locked," I say.

"Yes, it is." She picks up her knitting needles. "So, did you see anything else when you were canoeing?"

I tell her about the beautiful black and white bird who made the eerie sound.

Margaret smiles. "Your first loon."

CHAPTER SIXTEEN

"This is just like summer camp," I say.

We've had lunch (pancakes) but we're still at the kitchen table. Jane's making bracelets out of beads from a kit that Margaret gave her. She's been working on them all morning. I'm flipping through *The World of Origami Butterflies*, looking for the butterfly that has the fewest steps.

"This is Arts and Crafts," I say. "I went canoeing yesterday and tomorrow we're going horseback riding. Maybe Margaret will teach us archery too."

"I don't think so." Jane holds up a bracelet made out of purple and orange beads. "This one's for Margaret. I'm making yours next."

Margaret, who already has at least six bracelets on each arm, is asleep in the living room. Bella's outside. We haven't seen Wayne.

I turn pages. Twenty-two steps…twenty-four.

Forget it.

Nine.

I study a purple butterfly, perched on a glossy green bush. *Nine* steps. I choose a square of pale pink paper from the little box.

Jane's sorting through the beads. She's a bracelet factory. "What colors do you want?"

"Blue and green. Don't talk to me. I need to concentrate."

I'm okay until I get to *inverse reverse fold*. It's a tongue twister. How did Mom do this? I scrunch the paper into a ball.

"Why did you do that?" says Jane.

"Because I quit."

~

In the morning, Margaret says, "Wayne's having his coffee on the verandah. Why don't you girls take your breakfast outside and join him. He'd like that."

Jane's pouring Rice Krispies into a bowl. She stops and looks at me. Her eyes are huge. I grab the cereal box before Rice Krispies spill all over the counter. "Okay," I say.

I get a bowl of cereal for myself and head out to the verandah. Jane comes too, but she sticks close behind me. She goes straight to the stairs that lead down to the grass and sits on the top step. She turns her head quickly and peeks at Wayne, who's sitting in an armchair near the Butterfly House. Then she starts shoveling down Rice Krispies.

I sit down in the chair next to Wayne. "Hi," I say.

He nods. He's holding a coffee mug in both hands. His knuckles are swollen and red. He's wearing a different plaid shirt but the same belt with the huge silver buckle. His two canes are leaning against the back of his chair. He lifts the mug slowly to his mouth and holds it there, taking sips. I eat my cereal. We're both watching Jane, who's jumped off the steps and is rolling around on the grass.

"Where's Bella?" he says. "Why isn't Bella out here?"

"Jane's afraid of dogs."

"Why on earth is she afraid of dogs?"

I'm not going into all that again. "She just is."

Wayne lowers his mug and sets it shakily on a little table in front of him. It almost tips and coffee sloshes out. I concentrate on eating.

"I looked for your mother," he says. "I looked everywhere."

My stomach flips over. I put my spoonful of cereal back in the bowl. I'm done.

"Layla just disappeared one morning. She must have walked to the highway and hitchhiked. She went to Calgary. We didn't know that at first." He breathes in loudly.

Calgary, where I was born. Where I lived until I was four years old.

"I went to Vancouver and then I found out about Calgary, and I went there." He's gasping. He's using up all his energy to tell me this. "And I went back and back to Vancouver. I talked to everyone. The police, people that knew her. I spent months searching for her. We even put missing person notices in the newspaper. Nothing. She was supposed to start at Simon Fraser University in Vancouver that January. I went back down to

Vancouver. I went to the campus every day for two weeks. But all that time she was in Calgary."

I've heard enough. I jump up. "I don't care. I'm sorry you wasted all your precious time, but I wasn't even born. It's got nothing to do with me."

"Don't you come waltzing in here—"

"Are you *deaf* too? I told you, I don't give a shit about how hard you looked."

I have no idea why I'm yelling at him. I don't even know why I'm so mad but my heart's pounding like crazy.

"You listen to me, girlie!" Wayne bends over. He can't breathe. I've pissed him off and now he's dying.

I run to the door. "Margaret!"

She's there in a second, looks at Wayne, and says quietly, "I'll get the wheelchair."

She does everything calmly. She sets the brakes on the wheelchair, wraps her arms around Wayne's chest and helps him shift out of his chair and onto the seat of the wheelchair. I stand back, frozen, while Margaret unfolds a blanket and lays it across his knees.

"I'll take you inside," she says. "You okay, Rachel?"

I nod.

But I'm not okay. I'm shaking.

Wayne turns his head and looks at me. "I did what I had to do. I had no choice."

What the hell does that mean?

"Hey, Rachel!" shouts Jane. "Look at me!"

She's climbed into a striped hammock hanging between two trees and she's rocking it back and forth.

"Make room for me," I say.

If I were looking for Jane, I'd never give up. I'd keep looking forever.

~

I'm inside the Butterfly House, looking at Stephanie's butterfly. It's different from the other butterflies. Way more complicated. More delicate. This might have been the last butterfly Mom made. She'd have been really good at making butterflies by then. An expert. A butterfly factory.

I blow softly and the white butterfly spins.

Who is Stephanie?

~

Last night, I slept for two hours and forty-seven minutes. GoToSleep.com says you get way more sleep than you think you do because you're actually sleeping when you think you're awake. Not true. That's what people who've never had insomnia say to make us feel better. I know exactly how much sleep I get every night.

Aura has forbidden me to google, Can you die from sleep deprivation? *Not* helpful, she said.

Last night was Jane's fault. Margaret was in her bedroom with her door open, and I couldn't get past her to get a clean set of sheets. I'd just turned out the light when Jane said the plastic mattress cover was too slippery without a sheet.

We traded bunks.

Then Jane said she couldn't sleep so close to the ceiling because there wasn't enough air.

We traded bunks.

I pulled the sheet off my bunk and put it on the plastic mattress cover. By then it didn't matter if I had any sheets because I was wide awake.

Margaret heard me in the kitchen. There was exactly one mug of warm cocoa left in the pot on the woodstove, which I drank while I read the list of ingredients on the box of Rice Krispies.

"Come outside for a minute," she said.

I followed her out to the verandah with my cocoa. I stopped, stunned. The sky was a black bowl brimming with stars. Billions of stars. Margaret showed me the Milky Way and how to find the Big Dipper.

Stars don't all look the same. I didn't know that. Some are bright and some are faint and some really twinkle like stars are supposed to.

We didn't talk.

Just gazed and gazed at stars.

CHAPTER SEVENTEEN

I'm inside the barn.

It's made out of logs. A cement aisle runs down the middle with four stalls on each side. In two of the stalls, wood shavings are scattered on the floor and a black bucket hangs on the wall.

It smells nice in here. Maybe like hay?

There are wooden signs above each stall door with a name burnt into the wood. The stalls with the straw belong to Dancer and Magic. I read the other names. Skipper. Ben. Sadie. Montana. Choco. Tippy. Margaret says they only use the barn in the winter. I try to imagine blowing snow and howling wind and the horses munching hay in their stalls. Now there's only Dancer and Magic. I wonder if they get lonely.

A door at the end of the barn opens into a small room that Margaret calls the tack room. Along the walls are racks with saddles. Bridles hang from hooks and a high wooden bench is cluttered with plastic bottles of *Mane Detangler* and *Horse Shampoo*, sponges, a big tin that says *Fly Spray*, and bins full of brushes.

I dig through a trunk of dusty cowboy boots and pull out boots that might fit me. They have scrolly designs on the sides and pointed toes and they don't look like they're going to be comfortable. I finally find a worn pair that fit and feel good. Under the dust, the leather is dark red. Jane already has her boots. She's been clomping around in them since yesterday.

Somehow Margaret talked me into this. I'll ride once and never again. Like I told Amber, it's not my thing.

I go back outside. Margaret's tying a pony with black and white splotches to a long wooden rail beside two big horses. They're all swishing their tails at flies.

"The black horse is Magic," says Margaret. "That's who you're riding, Rachel. Magic was your mom's horse."

This is information I don't need right now.

"I want to ride Mom's horse," says Jane.

"No, you're riding Dixie. Magic is for Rachel."

I think she's waiting for me to say something, but I don't.

Margaret hands out plastic things called curry combs and dandy brushes. She demonstrates on Dancer who's tall and golden brown. You use the curry comb first, which stirs up a cloud of dust and dirt, and then the dandy brush. You start at the neck and work backwards. And you have to do all this without getting stomped on.

The sun's warm on my back and Magic smells nice. I think he's fallen asleep. He has one white foot, a white stripe on his face, and very long eyelashes. By the time I'm finished, his coat isn't exactly gleaming, but he doesn't look quite so dirty. Margaret picks up each of his hooves and cleans it with a pointed metal thing called a hoof pick. Then it's time to put the saddle on.

A square blanket goes first and then the saddle. Magic grunts when Margaret tightens the latigo, which is the strap that goes under his belly. The bridle's next. It looks complicated, with lots of straps and buckles, but Margaret slips it over Magic's ears easily and he opens his mouth for the silver bit.

She unties him and hands me his reins. "Always mount on the left side. It's got something to do with the way knights carried their swords."

Margaret helps Jane get on Dixie. I grab onto the horn (the thing that juts up at the front of the saddle), put my boot in the stirrup, and try to pull myself up. The saddle slides toward me and Magic's ears flick backwards. "Sorry," I mutter, shoving the saddle back.

"Try to spring up," says Margaret.

I spring.

I shove the saddle back in place.

"Give a little hop," Margaret suggests.

I make it on my third hop. As I slip my feet into the stirrups, Margaret adjusts the length of the stirrups on Dixie's saddle. She glances at me. "Your stirrups look about right. Do you feel balanced?"

"Yes." I take a deep breath and pick up the reins.

"Are we going to gallop?" says Jane.

"No." Margaret swings up on Dancer and picks up Dixie's lead rope. "Everyone ready? Let's go."

~

We ride along the gravel driveway, Margaret and Dancer in the lead, Jane and Dixie in the middle, and Magic and me clomping along last. After a few minutes, we turn on to a narrow grassy lane that disappears into the forest.

So far, I've been hanging onto the saddle horn but now I let go. Horseback riding is actually not that difficult. I even let myself look around. There are patches of shade and sun all through the trees and carpets of the same blue flowers we saw in the logged-out area.

Then we're back out of the trees at the end of a grassy meadow. It's marshy on one side, water glinting between tall weeds and bulrushes. Five Canada geese are swimming in a row with their heads high, ducking in and out of the reeds. It's like Lost Lagoon in Stanley Park but it doesn't end. It keeps going as far as I can see, maybe even to that far away ridge of trees.

Facing the marsh, an old log house is sinking into the grass. The logs are almost black. The roof has gaping holes and is covered with patches of lime green and gray moss. Sunlight glints on the glass in a small window under the eaves. There's no glass in any of the other windows, and birds are swooping in and out.

We ride right up to the door, which is hanging open on one hinge. I can see an old black woodstove leaning to the side and splattered with bird poop, and a narrow, steep wooden staircase.

"Wayne was born in this house," says Margaret. "This is part of the old Bird homestead. There were some other buildings, a barn, a milking shed, and a little bunkhouse, but they're all gone. The barn was moved. The other buildings just fell apart and the logs that hadn't rotted were used for other things. Somehow this house has managed to still be here." She smiles. "Like the Birds."

"Who lives here now?" says Jane.

"Just the barn swallows," says Margaret. "They've made nests inside on the rafters. Rows and rows of mud nests. One year, some of our cows got in. They were trying to escape the flies. They made a terrible mess."

"How old is it?" I ask.

"Daryl and Daphne Bird built it in 1917. So, well over a hundred years. Wayne's father, Joseph Bird, was born here too. He was your great-grandfather. He and your great-grandmother, Mary Bird, kept the place going and looked after Wayne and his three sisters and the cattle here. All those cold winters! Fifty below was normal in those days."

"Did you know Daphne and Mary?" says Jane.

"I knew Mary. Joseph and Mary were married shortly after the war, and they struggled for a long time to make ends meet. But Joseph was finally able to build our house where we all live now, and the family moved up there. Wayne was fourteen. He still calls it 'the new house' and except for the green metal roof, it hasn't changed much. It's over fifty years old now!"

"Can we go inside here?" says Jane.

"Not right now. But you girls can come back and look around if you like. You'll have to climb over that broken down snake fence over there. If you don't mind walking through nettles, it's only ten minutes from our house. We've just taken a longer route on the horses."

As we ride away, Margaret says, "You can explore the main floor, but you won't find much. But absolutely no going up the stairs. That's Wayne's rule. He's afraid they might cave in. Even worse, the upstairs floor could collapse."

"It won't," says Jane.

"It might," says Margaret.

"That's not fair," says Jane.

"Your uncles and your mother weren't allowed to, either."

"They never ever went up there?"

"Never," says Margaret. "Wayne was very strict."

"What's up there?" Jane persists.

"Nothing. Just a couple of empty rooms."

"Please, please, please, Margaret?"

"No. It's not safe."

Margaret turns in her saddle.

"Why are you looking at *me*?" I say.

~

We've come to a field with a gate. Margaret reaches down and opens it without getting off Dancer. Smooth. I go through first. Then Margaret and Dancer and Jane and Dixie scoot through. Margaret closes the gate, and we start across the field.

The grass is up to Magic's belly, and he keeps stopping and snatching mouthfuls. He's starving. But he's probably not supposed to do this. Horse rules. And besides, we're getting way behind.

Margaret and Jane are waiting at the end of the field at another gate.

"Give him a little kick," Margaret calls out.

Kick Magic and let him think he should gallop to catch up? I pretend I don't hear her. When we leave the field, we ride along another grassy road, and then we're back on a trail that winds through trees with scraggly gray moss hanging from the branches. It's shady and cooler out of the sun. Magic loves this part. His ears go forward, and he clops along happily behind Dixie.

Next, we ride through part of the forest where fallen trees with black trunks are piled up like pick-up sticks. Margaret talks about pine beetle again, and climate change, but I only half listen. The horses scoot down a dip in the trail and then they scramble up a bank, step over a log, and come out into a meadow with an open grassy hillside at the far end.

"When are we having the picnic?" says Jane.

Margaret's packed food in a leather bag hanging from her saddle. "We'll go right to the top of that hill," she says. "There's a nice spot up there beside a big flat rock we can use for a table."

The horses lunge up the hill, and Jane screams, and I grab the saddle horn. At the top, you can see forever—fields bordered with woods, the old Bird homestead by the marsh, the green metal roof of Wayne and Margaret's house, scattered buildings, the lake.

Getting off is way easier than getting on. I half-slide, half-jump to the ground. I copy Margaret and hook the reins to the saddle so Magic can graze without stepping on them.

She unpacks the food and sets it out on the rock: buns, cheese slices, oatmeal cookies, blueberry muffins, watermelon, and oranges. "For the vitamin C so we don't get scurvy," she says.

"This is dinner, right?" Jane can't believe her luck.

"Yes, it's dinner," says Margaret. "It's too hot to light the woodstove and cook anything."

I get my water bottle from the saddle bag and take a big gulp, as a boat cuts across the lake below, leaving a strip of white wake behind it. I sit on the grass, stretch my legs out, and eat a muffin.

Jane devours at least six cookies and wanders away, picking yellow flowers.

Now that Magic's allowed to eat grass, he's changed his mind. His head's hanging down and he's not moving.

"Hey, Magic," I say, and one of his long black ears swivels toward me.

Every time I say "Magic," he swivels his ear. I'm probably starting to annoy him, so I prop myself up on my elbow and just watch. He's on fly alert. When one lands on his back, he swishes his tail. When one lands on his leg, he stamps his foot. Flies on his face? His ears flick back and forth, and he shakes his mane.

It's quiet, except for the jingling of Dancer's and Dixie's bridles as they roam about, tearing up grass. It's peaceful.

I can't hear Jane.

I look around. I can't see her either and Margaret's leaning back against the rock and could be asleep. I leap up. "Where's Jane?"

"Don't worry, I've got my eye on her," says Margaret. "She's just over there by those trees."

Jane's dragging something that looks heavy. She shouts at us. Margaret stands up, too. "Let's go see what she's found."

It turns out she's found some kind of head, which is attached to a rib cage, which is attached to what looks like a leg. An entire dead animal. Clumps of brown hair and flesh are hanging off the bones.

"Jesus, Jane!" I say. "That stinks!"

"What is it?" she says.

"It's a deer." Margaret's laughing.

"Why is it dead?"

"Hard to say," says Margaret. "Maybe wolves killed it. Or coyotes. Or a bear."

More bones are scattered in the long grass. Jane piles them up. "I'm collecting bones!" she announces. "From now on."

"You can bring three bones back to the house," says Margaret. "But they can't have flesh on them, and they can't be too big. We'll tie them on my saddle."

Oh my God. We're all going to get some horrible disease. Jane will have to have a bath in hand sanitizer every day for the rest of her life.

CHAPTER EIGHTEEN

When I stagger down for breakfast at ten o'clock, Margaret and Jane are at the table, hunched over a piece of paper.

"Chinese food!" says Jane. "I forgot to say Chinese food! Write it down. Please, please, please!"

Margaret picks up a pen. "Okay, but that's plenty. We can work with this."

"Look, Rachel!" says Jane.

There's a line down the middle of the paper and two lists.

JANE'S FAVORITE FOODS
Hot dogs
Pizza Hut pizza
Ketchup chips
Fruit Loops
Kraft Dinner

Pancakes
Chicken fingers
McDonald's french fries
Jam sandwiches
Alphaghetti
Chinese food

MARGARET'S FAVORITE FOODS
Meatloaf
Pepper steak
Broccoli and beef stir fry
Chicken pot pie
Shepherd's pie
Steak burritos
Roast lamb
Pork sausages

Jane is clearly a junk food addict. Margaret's a carnivore. So far, Wayne just eats eggs.

I drop a piece of bread in the toaster. "I'm going to skip the vegetarian stage," I say, "and go straight to vegan."

~

Finally! Jason and I are communicating!

ME: There are BILLIONS of stars here.

JASON: There are BILLIONS of stars in Van too. You can't see them because of all the city lights.

ME: Thanx Einstein.

~

Margaret, Jane, and I are in the living room. Wayne's in his lair. Margaret's knitting and Jane's sorting out the *Nate the Great* books she dragged back from the shed. I'm reading my kindle, *The Amber Spyglass* by Philip Pullman. I'm dreading going to bed.

BANG! CRASH! Jane leaps up and I follow her to the window. Something seriously scary is happening outside. Margaret turns on the outdoor light.

"OH MY GOD!" yells Jane.

A huge black bear is on the rampage—right here in front of us on THIS VERANDAH! He has an enormous head and tiny, mean eyes. There's a very thin pane of glass between him and us.

He smashes into the table, which flips on its side.

Jane screams.

Wayne thumps into the living room, his canes banging on the floor. "What the hell's going on?"

"Bear," says Margaret. "He'll leave when he sees there's nothing to eat."

I wince as the bear rips his deadly claws right through the back of the old armchair. Stuffing pours out. My heart flips over. The Butterfly House. Please don't destroy the Butterfly House.

Another minute and the bear bounds off the verandah with a *woof* and disappears into the night. Bella's barking like crazy in the laundry room. I take a few deep breaths.

"He's gone," says Margaret.

My legs are like jelly.

The sooner Jane and I get out of here, the better.

~

PLAN D: WALK TO THE HIGHWAY AND HITCHHIKE TO HUNDRED MILE. ASAP.

~

3 A.M.

I'm in the laundry room, stuffing three damp sheets into the washing machine. I can't keep swiping new sheets. Margaret will catch me for sure. I figure I can wash these ones tonight because her bedroom door is closed and she's a mile away.

In laundromats, the washing machines are gross with soap scum from the last person, and you always run out of loonies before you've finished drying everything. This washing machine is clean. I pour Mrs. Meyer's Clean Day Laundry Detergent into the little plastic drawer on top of the machine. When I press the *start* button, a row of tiny red lights blink. High tech. I even have options: *stain cleaner, fresh water rinse*. I choose *energy saver* because it sounds the fastest. The washing machine rumbles, water whooshes in and—shit! It's crashing and bumping and banging like it's going to take off any second.

I jam my thumb on *stop* but it doesn't stop.

"What the hell are you doing?" says Wayne.

I spin around. He's in the doorway in blue striped pajamas and an old brown cardigan, leaning on his canes.

"Laundry," I say.

We stare at each other.

"Follow me," he says.

~

There's a door next to the laundry room that looks like it could be a closet for brooms and cleaning stuff. It's Wayne's room. It's crowded with his bed, a saggy armchair, a night table with a row of pill bottles, an ancient looking desk with an old type-writer sitting in the middle of scattered papers. Books are piled everywhere and, all around the walls, cardboard boxes stuffed full of filing folders are lined up. It's gotta be a hundred degrees in here. Bella's stretched out on a blanket beside the bed. She thumps her tail, but she doesn't raise her head.

Wayne lowers himself into the armchair. "I bet you want to leave," he says. "Get out of this place. Get back to all your boyfriends in Vancouver."

"You got that right," I say.

The washing machine screeches. I'm giving Wayne twenty seconds to tell me what he wants.

"We'll make a deal," he says. "I'll take you to the bus depot in Hundred Mile."

"And how will you do that?"

"I'll drive you."

"You can drive? No one took your license away?"

"You're damn right I can drive."

"And you really think Margaret will let you?"

"She won't know until it's too late. We'll go next Friday. Susan's picking her up and they're going to Kamloops for Susan's physio appointment. Susan likes it when Margaret goes with her. They'll be gone for hours."

That's the kind of scheme I'd come up with. "So, what's the deal?" I say. "What do I have to do?"

"Find something," he says. "A yellow and white envelope. I filed it somewhere. It could be between some papers. I was tired. Maybe I was sick. I don't remember but I can't find it. It's one of those envelopes that photos come in. You know what they look like."

Nope. Any photos Mom ever took stayed on her phone.

I glance around. "What is all this stuff?"

"My research. Notes. I'm writing the history of the Bird Family. *Our* family."

If that's supposed to mean something to me, it doesn't. I have no desire to be part of this family.

"So, I'm supposed to find this envelope in all this mess?"

"Watch your tongue, girlie. Deal or no deal?"

This is so crazy it might just work.

"Deal," I say.

As I leave his room, he says, "There's one more thing. You can't tell Margaret. Never."

~

I pull the wet sheets out of the washing machine, sloshing in my socks through a pool of water that's leaked onto the floor. So much for high tech.

I twirl in a complete circle, looking for the dryer.

What kind of laundry room doesn't have a dryer?

I remember seeing a row of blue jeans and plaid shirts flapping in the breeze on the clothesline beside the garden.

I shove the wet sheets back into the garbage bag and go.

~

PLAN E: ESCAPE TO HUNDRED MILE IN WAYNE'S GETAWAY TRUCK.

~

I now have two garbage bags with sheets. Wet, clean sheets and wet, peed-on sheets.

~

"Jane wants to go riding this morning," says Margaret. "Would you like to come with us?"

I glance up from my book. "No, thank you," I say automatically. "I'll stay here."

Is that what I really want?

Yes, that's what I really want.

CHAPTER NINETEEN

Margaret, Jane, and I pile into the pickup truck and drive to the store. Margaret wants to check her mailbox and get some milk. A sign hanging over the verandah says *Aspen Lake General Store Est. 1920*. There's a gas pump out front, some droopy hanging baskets, a long wooden bench, and a huge bulletin board covered with notices beside the door.

When we go inside, a man at the counter glances up from a car magazine and says, "Oh, hi there, Margaret."

"Hello, Lucas."

He slaps his magazine shut and stands up. "There's a parcel you've got to sign for."

"You girls see if there's anything you want," says Margaret. She and Lucas go to the back of the store where there's a big red and white sign saying Canada Post and a wall of silver mailboxes.

On the way here, Margaret told Jane she could pick one fun cereal. Jane finds the shelves of cereal boxes in two seconds, and I leave her agonizing between Chocolate Lucky Charms and Cinnamon Toast Crunch, neither of which she's ever tasted.

I wander. This store is super cluttered. There's the usual food—shelves of cans and jars and plastic bags of bread and hot dog buns. You can buy T-shirts, mops, brooms, baseball caps, a winemaking kit, a Styrofoam cooler, Band-Aids, bug spray, a patio umbrella, mugs that say *I'd Rather be Fishing*, a set of frying pans. You could survive for years on the stuff in here.

I check out a rack of books but there's nothing I want to read. They're all stories about pioneers or ghost towns or working on the Canadian Pacific Railway a million years ago. Maybe Wayne plans to sell his book here. If there ever is a book.

I go outside and sit on the bench. A blue pickup pulls in, stops, and then backs up to a shed with a big open door. A woman gets out of the truck and jumps up in the back. She's tossed six plastic sacks full of pop cans onto the ground when a boy comes out of the shed. He's got a dark tan, shaggy blond hair, and he's wearing faded jeans and a black T-shirt.

He takes the sacks inside the shed, three at a time, and then the woman starts handing down cases of beer bottles. She's an alcoholic or she's been saving bottles for ages. When she finally leaves, she calls out the window, "Thanks, Cody! Take it off my tab!" He waves and picks up the last two cases of bottles.

A truck pulling a humongous trailer arrives, aiming for the gas pump. A man is driving, and a woman gets out and stands by the pump and starts hollering directions. He tries to maneuver in.

Cody walks over. He smiles at me. I'm not fast enough. It's too late to smile back because he's pulling out the nozzle for the gas. The man finally gets his truck close enough and he and the woman disappear inside the store, arguing about something.

"Fancy rig," says Cody, looking up at me while he pumps the gas.

"Yeah," I say.

He glances over at Margaret's truck. "Are you with Margaret Bird?"

"Yup."

"Your grandmother, right?"

I try not to look surprised. "Yes."

"I heard you were coming to Aspen Lake. I'm Cody."

Who did he hear that from?

"I'm Rachel."

Cody clicks the nozzle a few times, checks the amount on the pump, and then pulls the nozzle out and slides it back into its holder. This gives me fifteen seconds to think of something incredibly interesting to say. What's wrong with me? I'm totally tongue-tied.

"How do you like it here?" he says.

"It's okay."

Margaret and Jane come out of the store just then. Margaret looks at me and she looks at Cody.

"Hi, Margaret," says Cody.

Margaret nods. "Come on, Rachel," she says. "I need to get back."

Something's bugging her. Get back for what? To feed Bella? To feed Wayne? To weed the garden?

"I'll see you around," says Cody. "Are you going to the rodeo?"

"What rodeo?" I say, but then Margaret honks the horn because, all of a sudden, she's in such a big hurry.

"You should go," says Cody. "It's a lot of fun."

~

1 A.M.

I'm in my bunk, reading my kindle. It has its own little light, so I won't wake up Jane. I've just about finished *The Amber Spyglass*. I have 13% left, which is not nearly as satisfying as real pages in a real book. I turn it off. I'd kill for some cocoa but I'm not going downstairs.

I think about Cody again.

I think I'm supposed to be thinking about Jason. I do think about him but right now I'm thinking about Cody. And I don't want to feel guilty about Jason.

My longest sentence was two words. Why did I get so flustered?

I wonder when this rodeo is. And how I can get to it.

If I'm still here, that is.

CHAPTER TWENTY

The phone rings at breakfast. *Two* rings. Ten seconds of silence. One ring. Not Uncle Rob this time. Another secret code?

Margaret picks it up. "Hello, Susan."

Amber's mom.

"They're settling in very well." A pause.

"Yes, I'll speak to her." Another, slightly longer pause. And then, "Hello, Amber…around one o'clock…? That would be fine. Cassie can stay all afternoon. Jane will love that."

I pull the plug and the water swirls away.

The thing about Amber? She talks too much.

~

In the afternoon, Amber trots up the driveway on a huge white horse, Cassie perched behind her.

"Hi, Jane!" Cassie shouts.

Jane's gripping my hand, and her mouth is clamped shut. She's been watching out the window for Cassie since lunchtime but she's nervous. She's way better at talking to adults than kids her age.

Cassie slides off. She's chubby and covered in freckles like Amber. She has a pink backpack.

"What's that?" she says, staring at Jane's arm.

"My burn," says Jane.

"Oh," says Cassie. "Grandma said you've got a pony!"

"Her name's Dixie," mumbles Jane.

I poke her.

"Do you want to see her?" Jane says.

"Sure!"

They race off to the field where the horses are grazing.

"They'll be fine," says Amber. "I could hang around for a while—"

"I gotta to do some stuff with Wayne," I say.

"Wayne? Really?"

"Yeah."

"Okay then. Next time."

I glance over to the field. I see the horses but no Jane or Cassie.

"Over there," says Amber, pointing to a huge haystack on the other side of the fence. Cassie and Jane have climbed to the top and they're pulling stuff out of the pink backpack.

Amber picks up her reins. "They're gonna be clones," she says.

~

"Bring some of them over here and I'll look too," says Wayne.

I put a fat file folder on his lap. He knocks it with his hand and yellow pages covered with handwriting fly everywhere. He's silent while I scoop them up.

The top sheet is a map with the name *South Cariboo* at the top. It's a maze of rivers and hundreds of lakes with dotted lines meandering everywhere. The paper underneath is a list of supplies:

Sugar 200 pounds
Flour 300 pounds
Dried potatoes 20 pounds
Beans 60 pounds
Bacon 150 pounds
Lard 20 pounds

There's more on the back. Soap, cornmeal, salt pork, yeast....

"Let me see that," says Wayne.

I pass him the list. "They had to pack all that in on horseback," he says. "They had tough horses then. The men were tough, too. Your great-great-grandfather, Daryl Bird, came all the way from Texas to Saskatchewan; across the prairies and over the Rocky Mountains."

Wayne repeats a lot of his stories. I don't see any sign of a book yet. There's no computer and the typewriter is a dinosaur. I return to his desk, and he gives up trying to help. I've taken out all the file folders from the left drawer and rifled my hands through them, and I'm ready to tackle the right drawer. I don't want to even think about all the boxes.

This drawer is crammed with file folders too.

"You could be more diligent," he says. "Look a little harder."

I tilt the chair back. "Are you really writing a book about the Bird family?"

"You're damn right."

"Who's gonna want to read it?"

"Well, girlie, you young people might be addicted to your screens but there are people who still read books."

"I know. I'm one of them."

"Huh."

Back to work. I decide to leave the rest of the folders for now. I open the top left drawer. It's stuffed with bundles of recipe cards held together with elastic bands. The top card on each bundle is covered with the same handwriting as the yellow papers. With his swollen fingers…. How long has he been working on this book?

No yellow and white envelope tucked between the cards. It's hopeless. I haven't a clue why it's so important. Why Margaret can't know. There are photos inside it, obviously, but of what?

"So, what do you read?" he says.

I thought he was asleep. He's been so quiet.

"Fantasy." The other top drawer is easy because it's filled with pens, pencils, erasers, elastic bands, boxes of paper clips, and staples.

"Let me guess," he says. "*Harry Potter.*"

"Yup. But I've moved on."

"*Lord of the Rings.*"

"Ditto."

"I bet you skipped Elrond's Council. It's forty pages. Young people have no attention span these days."

"I read every word."

I slide my hand right to the back of the drawer. No envelope.

"No offense," I say, "but you don't seem like the *Lord of the Rings* type."

"I read the trilogy to your mother. When she was six."

My heart skips a beat. Mom read me the trilogy when I was six. Jane and I have finished *The Hobbit* and we're saving *The Fellowship of the Ring* until September.

This is when it's hardest, when I'm caught off guard.

Wayne closes his eyes. In under a minute, he's snoring. I'm sliding the drawer shut when I spot a key that's pushed up against the side. It's attached to a ring with a small cardboard label.

Jimmy's Yurt.

CHAPTER TWENTY-ONE

Margaret's going to the store to pick up the mail and buy some groceries. It's Friday. Computer day at the school.

"I can drop you off while I do the shopping," she says. "I could give you half an hour."

I have a new idea for my tattoo I want to google. Jane's keen to go because she just likes going places.

The school is next to the store, and it's much smaller than the schools in Vancouver. We go in through a side door. About a dozen computers are set up on desks in one of the classrooms. Some of the computers are taken. A group of girls who look about ten are crowded around a screen, giggling, and an older boy with a baseball cap on backwards is hunched over a keyboard, his fingers flying.

I set Jane up with games on an ancient-looking Mac and then sit down at the computer beside her. I take care of the important stuff first. The bus schedule—there's one every day to Vancouver. The rodeo—I find a Facebook page. I take a scrap of paper out of a wastepaper basket, find a pen beside the computer next to me, and write down the bus times and the date of the rodeo: July 12.

I've decided that Celtic knots are too ordinary. Everybody has them. I find a site on Norse mythology and look around for a while. I find something called a *Yggdrasil*. It's a sacred ash tree. It stands in the middle of the world and its branches stretch out over nine realms. It would make an amazing tattoo, but realistically? It would cost a fortune.

I google *yurt* and go to *Images*. I scan through rows and rows of different yurts. Some of them are fancy, with patterns on the walls and ceilings, and beautiful furniture and rugs. I linger longest on the black and white photos of traditional yurts in countries that end in *stan*—like Kazakhstan, Uzbekistan, Turkmenistan—where nomads live. These are real yurts.

I check on Jane. She's happy chasing rabbits down holes. I shut down the computer and wander into the hallway.

Thumps, shouts, and bangs are coming through two red double doors. One of the doors crashes open and a girl shoots out and skids over to a drinking fountain. I peek through the door into a small gym. A bunch of kids are racing around with hockey sticks. It's wild.

I see Cody.

He sees me, gives a quick wave, and dives after the puck. *Whack!*

"Yo, Cody! Over here!" someone yells.

I hang around for a minute. Cody's a great player. He's fast and he doesn't hog the puck. But he doesn't look at me again, and I'm staring so I leave.

I go into the front part of the school where there are more double doors, locked, and a wall of windows looking into a small library. That's what's missing in Aspen Lake. A public library.

Jane slides down the hall in her socks. "Margaret's here. We're going now. She says we can get ice cream!"

~

We eat our cones on the bench outside the store, so they won't melt in the truck.

"It'd be weird to go to such a small school for high school," I say.

"Oh, it's just an elementary school," says Margaret. "It goes up to grade seven. Rob and your mom and Jimmy went to Hundred Mile for high school."

"It's so far away."

Margaret wipes a drip off Jane's chin with a napkin. "Lick fast, Jane. Yes, it was a long way. Especially in the winter. They had to be out of bed by six. Leave in the dark and come home in the dark. But that's just what it's like for teenagers in Aspen Lake."

"Did you have to drive them every day?"

"They took the school bus. They caught it here at the store, so we had to drive them this far."

I have this sudden terrifying thought. What if I get stuck here and have to take the bus to Hundred Mile? Every day.

I don't even fall asleep until four o'clock in the morning. I picture myself in a coma stumbling out to the truck in the middle of a blizzard.

"And when they got their driving licenses in grade twelve," says Margaret, "Wayne let them take his truck to school sometimes, to give them a break. At first Uncle Rob, and then Uncle Jimmy and your mom."

"But Mom didn't drive."

"Whatever gave you that idea?" she says. "Of course, she drove. Jane, did you find anything fun to play on the computer?"

Margaret can do that at warp speed. Change the subject. Talk about something else. Like me. I throw my half-eaten cone in a garbage can and walk away.

I'm confused. This one time, Mom and Jane and I were waiting forever for the bus and we had grocery bags that weighed a ton and I said, "Why can't we have a car like everybody else?"

"Because we can't," said Mom.

"We could use it just for groceries and the laundromat," I said. "I'm sick of carrying all this stuff."

"Cars cost money, in case you haven't noticed," she said. She was pissed off.

I said, "Forget it."

But she wouldn't let it go. "Have you ever looked at gas prices?" she yelled.

By then, everyone was staring at us.

"Anyway," she said. "I don't have a license. I never learned to drive. I hate cars."

~

ME: In my next life, I'll live in Tajikistan.

AURA: Have you considered Outer Mongolia?

ME: Have you ever been to Tajikistan or Outer Mongolia?

JASON: Not on my bucket list.

~

I have to fight with the key, wiggling it back and forth. The padlock is rusty. It sticks. Then, with a little click, it pops open.

I'm inside.

The yurt is like I imagine a teepee would be, but way bigger. There's only that one window beside the door, but light filters in through a dusty skylight in the middle of the roof. There's not much furniture—a table with a laptop on it, a wooden chair, a saggy green couch with a plaid blanket draped over the back, a cot with a gray blanket folded at one end, a floor lamp. There's a woodstove with a pipe that disappears through a hole in the canvas wall, a tiny fridge, wooden cupboards.

Tangled red, yellow, and blue cords run around the edge of the floor. Margaret said that Uncle Jimmy had a generator for power.

It's cold.

Jimmy loved the yurt.

I imagine snow piling up over the skylight. You'd feel like you were buried alive in here.

The laptop is plugged into a yellow cord that disappears behind the fridge. Now this could come in handy. I could take it to the school and connect to the Internet.

Next, I open one of the cupboards. It's pretty bare. Flashlights, matches, candles, soap. One plate, one fork, one knife, one spoon, one cup. A pot. Another cupboard's full of binders, their spines labeled. *Grazing the grasslands. Sustainable cattle ranching. Raising beef cattle.*

I stand still for a moment, gazing around, trying to imagine Uncle Jimmy in here. It feels so lonely.

There's a big black Bible on a little table beside the bed, and words scrawled all over the wall. I walk closer to read them.

PSALMS 32: VERSE 4 FOR DAY AND NIGHT YOUR HAND WAS HEAVY ON ME, MY STRENGTH WAS SAPPED AS IN THE HEAT OF SUMMER.

The words are printed in black felt pen. There's a date, *August 2*. The year is just last summer.

AUGUST 10 HOSEA 5:15 THEN I WILL RETURN TO MY LAIR UNTIL THEY HAVE BORNE THEIR GUILT AND SEEK MY FACE IN THEIR MISERY THEY WILL EARNESTLY SEEK ME.

This is spooky. Who writes Bible verses on their walls? Crazy people? Religious fanatics?

AUGUST 16 JAMES 2:10 FOR WHOEVER KEEPS THE WHOLE LAW AND YET STUMBLES AT JUST ONE POINT IS GUILTY OF BREAKING ALL OF IT.

AUGUST 20 MICAH 7:19 YOU WILL AGAIN HAVE COMPASSION ON US, YOU WILL TREAD OUR SINS UNDERFOOT AND HURL ALL OUR INEQUITIES INTO THE DEPTHS OF THE SEA~

This one starts out clear like the others but by the time it gets to *you will tread our sins*, it's like he's lost control of the pen and it runs downhill and the word *sea* ends in a squiggle.

The last one is right above the bed. It's harder to read because there's a brownish mist all over it. Like someone sprayed it with dots of paint.

AUGUST 24 ROMANS 6:23 FOR THE WAGES OF SIN IS DEATH BUT THE GIFT OF GOD IS

He didn't finish it. Why? And what is that brown stuff?

I've got goosebumps on my arms. It's freezing in here. I want to get outside, back into the sun.

I do miss my laptop. I grab Uncle Jimmy's and the power cord and leave.

CHAPTER TWENTY-TWO

Jane and I cut up vegetables for toppings for Margaret's home-made pizza. They're early vegetables which means they come from Margaret's greenhouse. Red and green peppers, zucchini, and golden cherry tomatoes. Margaret rolls out the dough into three circles and spreads on her homemade pizza sauce. Time to assemble.

"Where's the pepperoni?" says Jane.

Margaret takes a small bowl filled with tiny discs of pepperoni out of the fridge. "Okay," she says. "One piece of vegetable for every piece of pepperoni."

Carrots count. Jane's finished pizza is a masterpiece of orange and pink circles.

Margaret and I load ours with the peppers, tomatoes, and zucchini. We could open a pizza palace.

~

Wayne joins us for dinner.

We have strawberry ice cream after the pizza. Wayne asks Margaret for coffee. He's feeling friendly tonight.

"Let me see your bones, young lady," he says to Jane. "I hear you're collecting bones."

Jane looks at me.

"I told Wayne about your bone collection," says Margaret. "You can get them. They're washed and they've dried out nicely in the sun."

Jane is speedy. She dumps her bones on the kitchen table. They're smooth and white. Wayne picks up the bone that's long and thin and slightly curved. "This is a rib from a deer," he says.

"Oh," says Jane.

Another of the bones is wide and flat. "A scapula," he says. He holds up the last bone. It's small and round and has brown hair hanging from one end. "This is part of a hoof."

Jane hasn't been able to make one more word come out of her mouth. She's staring at the bones like she's never seen them before.

"Rachel, in my room on the shelf behind the desk there's a small cardboard box," says Wayne. "Go and get it and bring it here."

That sounds like an order, but I can be nice if I want to. Bella's on Wayne's bed and she gives me a guilty woof. "I'll keep your secret," I say.

I give the box to Wayne and he opens it and lifts out a little skull. It fits in his palm. It's so fragile it looks like you would crush it if you breathed too hard. There are two tiny dark sockets where the eyes used to be.

"This is a sparrow's skull," says Wayne. "Would you like to have it, Jane?"

"Yes," she whispers.

~

JANE'S NEW FAVORITE FOODS
Chocolate Lucky Charms
Homemade pizza
Carrots from the garden

~

2 A.M.

Jane's going to kill me. But I've run out of sheets. I need help.

"I guessed," says Margaret, when I tell her.

"You did?"

"The sheet cupboard. It's getting bare."

"Right." Something heavy slides off my shoulders. "I don't know what to do about it."

"You don't have to do anything," she says.

"I always look after Jane."

"And you're so good at it, Rachel. But we can look after her together now. And she'll stop. You said she doesn't do it every night."

Margaret sets her knitting on the floor and stands up. "I want to show you something."

She goes upstairs and comes back with a tin box. She pushes Bella to the end of the couch and sits beside me. The lid is covered with yellow sunflowers. She lifts the lid and takes out a stack of Christmas cards.

"We started getting them the second Christmas after your mom left," she says. "We got one every year. I've kept them in order, with the first one on top. She didn't write anything, just her name, and there was no return address. I looked at the postmark and they came from Calgary at first and then from Vancouver. But look what was inside."

Margaret passes me the card from the top of the stack. There's a snowman on the front and the words *Merry Christmas*. Inside it says *Happy Holidays* and underneath, in my mom's handwriting, *Layla*. On the blank side, there's a photograph scotch-taped at the top and bottom. It's a baby with spikey red hair in a pink blanket. Underneath, *Rachel*.

I'm in every one of the cards. I go from a baby to a toddler and then a little kid. I recognize things in the photos—my stuffed cat, the swing set at the park, my Star Wars T-shirt.

And then there's me with a weird haircut and a second photo, a tiny wrinkled baby with *Jane* written underneath. There are two more cards with me and Jane and then no more.

"She stopped sending them four years ago," says Margaret. "I don't know why."

I think I do.

"That's when Jane's dad left. He was paying child support and he'd buy toys for Jane, and then he just disappeared. And we never had enough money after that."

"Oh, Rachel, we could have helped," says Margaret.

"Mom didn't like people helping us."

She puts the cards back in the box. "You didn't know about us," she says. "But we knew about you."

CHAPTER TWENTY-THREE

"I want to see those Christmas cards, too," says Jane.

Margaret brings the chocolate box down to the kitchen table where we're finishing breakfast.

Jane flips through the stack quickly until the cards with her photos start. She studies each one, then goes back to her baby picture. She stares at it, forgetting to eat her banana bread.

"I was beautiful," she says finally.

Margaret kisses the top of her head. Jane wriggles down from the table, grabs her banana bread, and heads outside.

~

I clip the top corners of a sheet to the clothesline with wooden clothes pegs, reel the line out a little further, and pull another damp sheet out of the laundry basket.

They billow and flap in the wind, like they're breathing.

They're the white sails of a huge ship. They're the white wings on Stephanie's butterfly.

Margaret says there is nothing that smells as nice as sheets dried in the sun.

~

We're walking back to the house. I'm carrying the plastic laundry basket, and Margaret has the box of clothes pegs.

She stops. "Look."

Jane and Wayne are on the grass in front of the verandah. Jane throws a red ball and Bella barks and chases after it. "Bella will do that forever," says Margaret.

Jane throws the ball again. And again. And again. Each time, Bella brings it back and drops it at her feet. Her tail waves like a flag.

And Jane doesn't freak out. That's the amazing part. How did Wayne do it?

~

I dreamed that Jason came to Aspen Lake. We decided that we're going to get married and run the ranch together. Wayne's going to be our foreman.

~

JASON: Are you there?

Three bars! The best so far.

ME: Yup.

JASON: Call me.

Oh God. I've become clairvoyant. He's coming to Aspen Lake.

JASON: Still there?

He can't come. What if he gets here and I decide I don't want to be his girlfriend (am I his girlfriend?) and then what would I do?

JASON: Call me.

So I do.
"I know what the saying on the bench really means," says Jason.
You cannot leave a place you've never been to.
It's stuck in my head.
"What?" I say.
"You gotta feel the bad stuff before you move on. You gotta talk about it."

"Okay," I say.

"So, I'm going to test it on you," he says. "My mom left us when I was seven. I go back and forth between my Nana and my dad. For the last four years, he's been in a maximum security prison in Stony Mountain near Winnipeg for armed robbery. He's just got parole and he's living with my aunt and uncle on their farm in northern Manitoba. I'm moving there next week to stay with him."

A loon dives. The sun is just about to dip behind the ridge of trees across the lake. The lake is melted copper.

"A farm sounds good," I say.

"Yup."

"Maybe they'll have ducks."

"Maybe."

"I know. You can milk the cows."

"Rachel."

"Okay, okay. My mom died in December of a drug overdose, but she wasn't a drug addict. It was just an accident. She went to a party one night and she didn't come home. She took some fentanyl and she died in the hospital. Jane and I didn't know until my Uncle Rob came to our school the next day."

That's what Aura said. It was an *accident*. It took me a long time to believe her.

I just realized something. Uncle Jimmy died of an accident too, with his hunting rifle. Two accidents in the Bird family.

"Where's your dad?" says Jason.

"Don't have one. I was born by Immaculate Conception. Like Jesus."

Here comes that carapace turtle shell thing that Aura says I have. I *am* trying but it's hard.

Jason sighs.

"He's never been in the picture. My mom was really young. Nineteen."

We talk for a few more minutes and the three bars jump to four, but I'm drained.

"We'll stay friends?" says Jason.

It might be hard. Manitoba's so far away and I'm not that much into social media. But I say, "For sure."

Suddenly, I feel sad. This is ridiculous. Now I'm wishing he was coming here after all. I think he's the nicest friend I've ever had.

When I paddle back to shore, I think about what just happened. I do feel lighter inside, like when I've been talking to Aura.

But I didn't tell Jason everything.

I didn't tell him what I did to Jane.

CHAPTER TWENTY-FOUR

Really early in the morning, I take Jane out in the canoe. She paddles in the bow and I paddle in the back. We're a team. As long as I don't paddle harder than her, we go straight.

Jane's talking non-stop about Cassie and I have to keep splashing her to remind her to paddle. Cassie's staying with her grandparents for a few more weeks. Jane played at their house yesterday, and she and Cassie are making a fort under the basement stairs, with an old bedspread for a door.

"Okay, far enough," I say.

Jane leans over the edge of the canoe and snaps off a lily pad. I take out my cell phone. Two bars.

A text from Aura: A photo of a huge room that's glittering with chandeliers and mirrors. A castle?

AURA: Hall of Mirrors at the Palace of Versailles. You'd love it!

ME: A good place 4 my next life?

The lake is pink and purple. A long quavering cry echoes across the water.

"What's that?" says Jane.

"Your first loon."

~

HOW TO MAKE YAM FRIES

1. Peel the yams with a vegetable peeler.

DON'T LET LITTLE SISTERS HANG THE CURLY PEELINGS ON THE DOG'S EARS. SHE'LL (THE DOG) RACE AROUND THE HOUSE LIKE SHE'S DEMENTED AND THEN PEE ON THE LIVING ROOM RUG.

2. Cut them in ¼ inch wedges.
3. Drizzle vegetable oil on them.
4. Place them on a greased baking sheet in an even layer so they get crispy on all sides.
5. Bake them for ten minutes at 400 degrees. Turn them over with a spatula and bake them for ten more minutes.
6. Sprinkle them with salt.

JANE'S ~~NEW~~ NEW FAVORITE FOODS
Chocolate lucky charms
Homemade pizza
Carrots from the garden
Strawberries from the garden
Raspberries from the garden
Cucumbers from the garden
Margaret's chicken pot pie
Margaret's meatloaf
Yam fries

~

Jane and I are on a mission. Saskatoon berry picking. Margaret says the best place for Saskatoon berries is the old Bird homestead. We're wearing jeans because of the nettles. I'm carrying an empty ice cream pail. It's just before lunch and it's already hot.

The old house looks like it's sunk deeper into the long grass. It's even more deserted today because there are no swallows flying in and out of the windows. We walk down to the edge of the marsh. Dragonflies are darting over the tops of the reeds, making a clicking sound, their wings shimmery blue in the sun. Three ducks with white cheeks swim in circles, then disappear into the grass. It's quiet. Even the mosquitoes are leaving us alone.

Jane spots something dangling from the top of a bulrush. She takes off her runners, and I roll up the bottoms of her jeans and she plunges in. She wades over to the bulrush, picks it up carefully and brings it back, cradled in her hands.

"What is it?" she says.

It's delicate, brittle looking, grayish brown. "I think it's some kind of preserved bug," I say.

I study it more closely. There's nothing inside it. "Maybe it's the just the shell of a dead bug. Whatever it is, it's a pretty good treasure. Keep it?"

"Can I?" says Jane.

~

We find a safe place for it on top of a stump near the door of the old house. Saskatoon bushes are growing all around the sides and back of the house. The berries are fat, almost black. Jane and I can't decide if they taste like blueberries. We fill the ice cream pail in no time.

Then we go inside the house.

The bottom floor is one big room. The floor is packed dirt, littered with broken floorboards, shards of glass from the windows, and dried up cow patties. There are a few cupboards along one side wall with peeling blue paint and the black woodstove, tilting crazily. No furniture. You have to walk carefully. Glass crunches under our feet. Bird shit is splattered everywhere.

"Look up," I say.

Swallow nests are lined up along the rafters like apartments. They're made of gray mud with a small round hole at one end.

Jane counts them. "Thirty-five," she says.

"Shhh," I say.

There's a faint peeping sound.

"Where are the mother swallows?" whispers Jane.

"Looking for food for their babies. They'll be back."

I walk over to the staircase. It's narrow with steep steps.

"Are we going up?" says Jane.

"Yup."

"Are we telling Margaret?"

"Nope. And I'm going first to test it."

"It's fine," I say when I'm three quarters of the way up. "You can come up now."

There's a little landing at the top of the stairs with two closed doors. I tug open the door on the right and gaze in at a big room. The floor is covered with dead leaves. A ragged piece of faded red-checked curtain hangs at the gaping window frame. I can see blue sky through a huge hole in the roof.

I walk over to the window. I'm at the front of the house, looking out at the marsh. This is where I would sleep. I could smell the marsh and look at stars through the hole in the roof and not care if I stayed awake all night.

"Rachel! There's someone living here!" yells Jane.

She's in the other room. It's small, at the back of the house. The window still has glass, and the ceiling is made of planks. Someone's left an old sleeping bag on the floor. The end is chewed and pieces of white stuffing are strewn everywhere. A kid's tea set, pink rosebuds, tiny cups, and a teapot sit on a wooden box. There's a yellow plastic crate full of books and a tin box with horses on the lid.

"Who lives here?" says Jane.

"Nobody," I say.

I look at the books. *Black Beauty*, *The Black Stallion*, *My Friend Flicka*. Bookplates inside the covers. *This book belongs to Layla Bird.*

I take the lid off the box. There's a piece of purple paper inside, with the same loopy handwriting. I read it out loud.

I, Layla Anne Bird and I, Stephanie Sarah Robertson do solemnly swear to be best friends forever on pain of death. We seal this with an oath of blood on August 23, 1995.

Layla Anne Bird
Stephanie Sarah Robertson

Witness: Buster

"Why did they do that?" asks Jane.

"It's like a pact. Mom wrote it. It says 1995, so she'd have been about nine or ten, I think. I bet Buster was a dog. This is Mom's stuff. This was kind of like her secret fort."

"Like me and Cassie are making under the stairs?"

"Just like that."

"Who's Buster?"

"A dog, maybe?"

"And who's Stephanie?"

"Mom's best friend."

CHAPTER TWENTY-FIVE

"Male and female dragonflies mate while they're flying," says Wayne. "The female puts her eggs on a plant and if she can't find one, she drops them in the water. A dragonfly starts as an egg, then it's a nymph, and then it's a dragonfly. Most of its life, it's a nymph. It lives underwater, and you won't see it unless you swim around ponds or the marsh with your eyes open."

"What does it look like?" says Jane. "How would I know if it's a dragonfly nymph?"

"It looks like a tiny alien. It has no wings and a crusty hump on its back. It swims around and sometimes eats other dragonfly nymphs. And then, when the weather is just right, it climbs up the stem of a plant. It sheds its skin and crawls out. That's what this is, Jane. The discarded shell of a dragonfly nymph."

Jane wants to hang her nymph in the Butterfly House. She holds it in her hand, and I try to tie a fine thread onto it.

It crumbles into dust.

"Blow," I say to Jane, and she blows.

"Good-bye, poor nymph," she says.

"It's happy now," I say. "It's going back to its marsh."

~

We're in the Butterfly House, and I'm showing Jane the white butterfly.

"It's beautiful," she says.

She leaves in search of Wayne, but I linger.

I found you, Stephanie.

What happened to you?

~

The Saskatoon berry pie is golden brown and crusted with sugar and cinnamon. Purple berry juice oozes out the sides. I wove the strips of pastry for the top. Jane crimped the edges with a fork.

We take almost-too-hot-to-eat slices of pie and glasses of milk outside to the grass and devour them.

We have purple fingers and white moustaches.

~

ME: Is it a good idea to cut a hole in the roof above your bed so you can look at the stars?

JASON: If you live in the Sahara Desert, yes. If you live in the Amazonian rainforest, no.

~

Jane's squatting at the edge of the long grass. She's poking at something with two sticks. I walk over to see what's going on.

A tiny mouse is flopped on its side, its head twisted backwards, and its tiny eyes staring at nothing. There's a hole in its stomach and there's blood.

"I found a dead mouse," says Jane without looking up.

"I see that."

"I think it ate a poisonous mushroom."

"Oh. Well, that could be it."

"I'm trying to get its leg bone out."

"Right. Okay, I'll see you later."

I don't want to bug her. This could be the beginning of a great career as a world-famous surgeon.

CHAPTER TWENTY-SIX

Margaret asks me to open a gate in the field where the horses are grazing. They've eaten down the grass and can move into the next pasture.

Dancer and Dixie are totally into this. As soon as I open the gate, they streak through. Dancer kicks up his back feet and whinnies. Dixie gets right down to business, tearing up mouthfuls of long grass.

But Magic doesn't do anything. He's standing far away beside the fence, and he's not moving.

"Hey, Magic!" I shout. "Come on! Grass!"

Nope. Not interested.

Ranch rule number one. Never open a gate that was closed and leave it open. Does that count here?

"Come on, Magic! Please! I don't have all day!"

He's looking at something in the distance or he's not looking at anything. I can't tell. But he's not coming.

I sigh and walk over. He turns his head and gazes at me with his huge brown eyes.

"What's the matter?" I say, trying to sound cross.

Then I see it. Wire, wrapped tightly around his back legs. Get Margaret, I think.

Then I think, deal with it.

I rest my hand on his shoulder, and he shivers, his skin rippling under my fingers. "It's okay, boy."

I examine the wire. It's a mess. Will he kick me if I try to untangle him?

I crouch down, watching his ears. Flattened ears is a sign that a horse is pissed off. Magic's ears prick forward and he gives this little nicker. I'm not imagining it.

I'm committed to saving him now.

I unwrap the wire carefully. It's smooth wire, not barbed. But it takes me a long time. When I finally get it all off, I check Magic's legs for blood or cuts. Nothing. I stand up and wind the wire into a coil. "What are you waiting for?" I say. "You can go now. Your buddies are getting all the best grass."

At the end, I have to walk through the gate and Magic follows me.

I hang the wire over a post and sit on the top rail of the fence and watch the horses. Bees drone in clumps of pink clover. I close my eyes, tip my face to the sun.

Damp breath on my hand. A gentle nudge.

I open my eyes. I stroke Magic's face and he lowers his head.

I think hard about it.

Then I take a big breath and I slide onto his back. I fall forward and wrap my arms around his neck. I press my face into his mane.

I breathe in his smell.

He stands very still but this time, not because of wire. His warmth melts into mine.

～

Do I still want to go back to Vancouver? What's there that I like? Uncle Rob, the library, Second Beach, and Wi-Fi. That's all I can think of.

Jason's gone to Manitoba.

So what's good about Aspen Lake?

Jane's happy. I'm dealing with no Internet. I'm dealing with Wayne. Cody sort of asked me to go to the rodeo. And it's nice not being the only one up in the middle of the night.

And, there's Magic.

～

PLAN F: STAY HERE. JUST UNTIL THE END OF THE SUMMER.

CHAPTER TWENTY-SEVEN

I don't need Wayne to help us escape anymore. Does that mean I don't have to look for the envelope? Is the deal off?

~

Wayne refuses to open his window, and I'm cooking. Using one of his elastic bands, I pull my hair into a ponytail.

"I'll keep looking," I say, "but I'd probably try way harder if I knew why you want to find these photos so badly."

He glares at me.

I glare back.

"That's none of your business," he says. "You should be more focused. You're not getting anywhere. You're just moving boxes around."

"That's not true. I'm organizing them. Why do you keep all this stuff?"

"I told you. It's family history."

I lift a stack of bundles of paper out of a box, each one stapled in the corner. "This doesn't look like family history."

"They're old tax returns. You never know when the tax people will come after you. There's a thing called auditing, you know."

"I know what auditing is. It's when you get caught cheating. You've got tons of these. You must be really scared. What did you do?"

"You listen to me, girlie. I didn't do anything. I've accounted for every penny I've ever earned. And, by the way, by the time I was your age I'd had two or three jobs. Hard jobs. Physical labor."

"Oh. Well, anyway, when they come to audit you, they'll see all this mess and run."

For a second, I think he's going to smile.

I sneeze.

"Dust," I say. "I'm allergic to your room."

~

I'm thinking, just *thinking*, of typing Wayne's story. That's if Uncle Jimmy's laptop works.

Margaret and Jane have disappeared somewhere. But I shut our bedroom before I pull the laptop out from under the bunk bed. I plug it in and sit on Jane's bunk bed, resting it on my knees.

I lift up the lid. It hums for a minute, then JIMMY BIRD and a long narrow box with the word *password* pop up on the screen.

Shit.

It's not a bad laptop. Maybe a little bit older than mine. But it's useless if I can't get into it. I push a button on the side and a little drawer slides out. There's a silver CD in it. Across the top in black felt pen someone has written THE YURT, SUMMER 2005.

~

I go back to the yurt because I have to find out what's on that CD. I need the laptop password.

This time it feels even colder inside. Lonelier. I glance over at the Bible verses scrawled across the canvas wall but I'm not going to read them again. They make me feel sick.

I just want to see if I can find Uncle Jimmy's passwords written down somewhere. Then I'll go. I don't believe in ghosts but somehow it feels like I'm invading his privacy. That he wouldn't want me to be here.

I check each drawer under the counter. Most of them are empty. I find a roll of tin foil, batteries, an instruction manual for the generator, duct tape, envelopes, and felt pens. I'm not even sure what I'm looking for. Where do most people keep their passwords?

Beside the fridge, there's a tall cupboard with a metal clasp and a locked padlock on the door. I didn't notice it before. Now I'm just being nosey, but I try the yurt key. It fits.

Jesus! It's full of guns.

Not exactly what I was expecting.

They're lined up against the back wall of the cupboard. Six of them. Long and narrow and made of gleaming dark metal and wood. I haven't a clue what kind they are. I've never known anybody who owned a gun. I've never even *seen* a gun before.

Was one of these the hunting rifle that Uncle Jimmy had his accident with? And what does an accident with a hunting rifle mean exactly? Did it just go off somehow?

And why do you need six guns to hunt?

You hear all the time about these guys who go berserk and shoot people in a school or a mosque or a mall. Turns out they always had a big stash of guns. Gun freaks.

Does having six guns make you a gun freak?

I'm about to close the cupboard when I notice on the back of the door in black felt pen:

ASPEN2929#
JyuRT
LB2005**

Passwords.

I take a photo with my phone. Then I close the cupboard and lock it.

I've got what I need.

~

1 A.M.

"The social workers blamed Mom," I say.

I'm lying on the old purple couch with Bella, listening to Margaret's clicking knitting needles.

"What happened exactly?" says Margaret.

"Mom had a phone call. She said someone she knew had died and that she'd be away for three or four days."

"She didn't say who?"

"No. She promised she'd be back before the first day of school. But she wouldn't tell us where she was going."

"And you didn't guess it was here because you didn't know anything about us," says Margaret.

"No. Mom said her phone might not work and if we had any problems we were supposed to go to Crystal's."

"That's the woman who lived in the apartment next door," says Margaret. "And there was an older woman too. Mrs. Gunty?"

"She had the apartment at the end of the hall. But there was no way Mom wanted Mrs. Gunty to know she was leaving us by ourselves. She thought Mrs. Gunty was always poking her nose into our business. She said she'd just make trouble. That's why...."

My heart's pounding. I adjust my story. Change what needs to be changed.

"Jane was making some Mr. Noodles and the kettle tipped over and she started screaming. I was in the living room. I ran to get Crystal but she'd gone out somewhere. So I got Mrs. Gunty."

"That was the right thing to do," says Margaret.

I shake my head. "I overreacted. Mom was furious. I should have called 911 myself. That's what Mrs. Gunty ended up doing. And then she reported us, and we had to go into foster care for two months. Mom said if I hadn't got Mrs. Gunty, we'd never have been taken away."

"That's not true. The moment you and Jane showed up at the hospital without an adult, and they couldn't get hold of a parent, someone would have called social services. Mrs. Gunty just did it first. You were fourteen, Rachel."

"I shouldn't have got her."

Margaret knits for a few minutes. "Tell me about the foster home."

"It was okay. They were nice to us. But it was...."

The back of my eyelids burn. I stare hard at the wall.

"It was stressful," I say finally, "because we didn't know when we'd get to go back to Mom."

"I know," says Margaret.

"Did *you* know Mom was coming here?" I say.

"No one knew," says Margaret. "She just arrived. I never even asked her how she found out that your Uncle Jimmy had died. It was just so amazing that she'd come."

I looked for your mother. I looked everywhere.

"What did Wayne do when he saw her? Was he furious at her?"

"Oh no. No. He hugged her. He wouldn't let go of her."

It's impossible to imagine.

"Were Mom and Uncle Jimmy close?"

"Of course they were close," says Margaret. "Maybe no one's ever told you. They were twins."

~

2 A.M.

I'm lying in my bunk, waiting for morning.

If I could ask Mom one question right now, this is what it would be:

What did this family do that made you leave?

~

3 A.M.

"Rachel!" says Jane. "What's that noise?"

"I don't know. Climb up here, kiddo."

She's up the ladder in a flash and under my blanket. Outside, there's the most incredible thing going on. Yipping and yodeling and high-pitched wailing. Like a choir gone crazy. It's beautiful and eerie at the same time.

"Are they lions?" whispers Jane.

"No. Maybe they're wolves."

It lasts at least twenty minutes.

"It's making me shiver," says Jane.

"Me too."

When it's finally quiet, Jane says, "I might as well just stay here now."

"No. Down you go. I'll tuck you back in."

I pull the blanket up to her chin.

"I wonder what it was." She's falling asleep. "I'll ask Wayne."

CHAPTER TWENTY-EIGHT

"Coyotes," says Wayne. "There's a pack living in the bottom hayfield. They sing like that when the moon's full. Other nights, too. To mark their territory or to show other packs how strong theirs is and that they're united in times of stress. Family is very important to coyotes. Sometimes it's to celebrate a kill."

"What do they kill?" says Jane.

"Deer."

"What happens to a deer when it's killed?"

"Well," says Wayne, "by the time Mother Nature gets finished with it, there's nothing left except the bones. The scavengers go after it first. Around here, that'd be coyotes, weasels, cougars, wolves. And if there's any flesh left, these little flesh-eating beetles called dermestids pick the carcass clean. Other animals chew on the bones too, to get the phosphorous and calcium they need."

"Excuse me but we *are* eating," I say.

Margaret made a delicious shepherd's pie even though she's not joining us. She's been in her room all afternoon, in the dark. I went in with tea, but she murmured for me to leave her.

"But they don't eat all the bones," says Jane. "Because I'm finding them first."

"Right," says Wayne. "Bones take a long time to disappear."

"Unless you cremate them," I say. "Then presto, they're gone."

In less than a second, Wayne's face turns beet red. "What's the matter with you?" he shouts.

My mouth has gone completely dry. "I'm sorry," I stammer. "I don't know why I said that."

"What's cremated?" says Jane.

It's what happens when you're dead and you don't want your body to be buried in the ground so worms can eat it. So it can rot. Cremated is what they did to Mom. Maybe to Uncle Jimmy, too.

"It's…nothing, Jane."

Wayne shoves his plate of shepherd's pie across the table.

"What's cremated?" says Jane again.

I wait until Wayne slams the door. Then I tell her.

~

I type ASPEN2929# into the box.

The password is incorrect. Try again.

I type JYURT.

The password is incorrect. Try again.
I type LB2005**.
The password is incorrect. Try again.

CHAPTER TWENTY-NINE

Margaret drops Jane and me off at the rodeo on her way to Hundred Mile. There was some problem with Wayne and we're late. Margaret gave me twenty bucks for admission and the concession stand. I pay for myself, Jane is free. We walk through the gate.

"Are you ready for some more rodeo action?" booms a voice.

There's a huge sand arena with bleachers down one side. Crowds of people. Zero shade. The smell of hotdogs nearly knocks me over. It's going to be hard to find Cody.

I don't know what people wear to rodeos. I finally decided on my oldest jeans, a pale blue T-shirt, and my new-old cowboy boots. Looking around, I should have worn one of those dusty cowboy hats in the tack room.

I'm trying to figure out where we can sit when Jane shouts, "Cassie! There's Cassie!"

Shit. They're ten feet away, halfway up the bleachers. Amber has a red cooler beside her. She and Cassie are wearing pink cowboy hats. Amber stands up and waves. "Rachel! Jane!"

I really don't want to hear Amber's stories about the good old days. Too late. She's moving the cooler, shifting over, making room on the bleachers. We climb up the side and then make our way over. Cassie grabs Jane's arm. I sit down beside Amber.

"First rodeo?" says Amber.

"Yup."

"You're gonna love it." She hands me a program. "And don't worry, you haven't missed any of the good stuff."

At the end of the arena, a horse and cowboy explode out of a gate. The horse twists and bucks, snapping the cowboy back and forth. Finally, the cowboy flies off and lands on his back on the ground. He gets up slowly and picks up his hat. His horse takes off, charging around the arena, bucking hard, and two men on black horses chase it.

"That's one big, strong, high kickin' bay. Give that cowboy a round of applause. That's all he'll be taking home today."

I spot a man with a microphone standing in a high wooden booth, looking down on the arena. He's wearing a white cowboy hat and a white jacket with fringes down the arms.

I follow along in the program. About ten more cowboys compete in Saddle Bronc, and then there's something called Breakaway Roping where two cowboys on horses try to rope a calf. The calf runs for its life. I'm absolutely on the calf's side. No one else is. I cheer inside my head every time a cowboy misses.

People carry trays of french fries, jumbo hot dogs, and cans of pop across the front of the bleachers. I keep my eyes open for Cody.

Jane's pestering for mini donuts. "Please, please, please?"

"No," I say.

"It's almost intermission," says Amber. She's trying to smear sunscreen on Cassie's face, who keeps wriggling away. "Then we'll fill up on some junk."

I frown.

"Chill, Rachel. It's a rodeo." She checks the program. "I'll go to the concession right after the Steer Wrestling."

By the intermission, I'm hot and thirsty.

"We got lots more ahead, so don't go away!" says the announcer. "Get yourself over to the Beer Garden if you're feeling the heat."

There's a stampede from the bleachers.

"Okay," says Amber. "I'll make the concession stand run now."

"Here," I say. "Margaret gave me some money."

Jane and Cassie go, too. I take out my water bottle and guard our places, watching all the people.

No Cody.

But I see someone I know. A woman called Kelsey. I've seen her at Amnesty International meetings in Vancouver. Amnesty International is a human rights thing that Mom was really into. Sometimes she took me and Jane to see films about Syrian refugees or women in Afghanistan or things like that. Kelsey and Mom seemed to know each other because they'd talk during the coffee breaks.

What's Kelsey doing here in Aspen Lake? She's squatting down in front of the bleachers, talking to someone. I recognize her by her frizzy black hair and her orange shawl. She must be cooking.

Cassie and Jane are back with a sack of mini donuts and powdered sugar all over their faces. Amber's carrying a giant poutine. She stops and says something to Kelsey. They talk for a minute, then Kelsey disappears into the crowd, and Amber climbs up and passes me the poutine over two empty bleachers.

"God, what a line up," she says, sitting down. "Everyone in Aspen Lake must be here. I just ran into Kelsey Rainer. She doesn't live here anymore, and I haven't seen her for eons. We used to have these Amnesty International meetings in their basement."

Kelsey's from Aspen Lake? That means that all this time, there was one person from Aspen Lake who knew that Mom was in Vancouver.

That means…what?

Jane's staring at the poutine. "What is *that*?" she says.

"Poutine," I say. "Fries, gravy, and cheese curds. That's what you eat when you want to have a heart attack."

It's bugging me, seeing Kelsey. I check the program to see what comes next. Junior Steer Riding.

I scan the list of contestants. Seven names. Number seven is Cody Cooper.

"Alright, folks, get ready for some action. Keep your eyes on chute number two. It's Jamie Martin from Williams Lake. Let's make some noise for Jamie!"

The gate crashes open. A steer bursts into the arena, giving a great twisting kick with his back legs. Jamie is clinging to a strap on its back. Three hard bucks and he soars through the air. I wince. The crowd groans, and Jamie stands up and dusts off his legs.

"No score for Jamie," says the announcer. "Give him a hand, folks. That ground comes up mighty hard."

"You have to stay on eight seconds to get a score," says Amber.

Eight seconds. Forever.

∼

"Listen up, folks. We're at chute number three now. Our last contestant. A young cowboy, Cody Cooper, from right here in Aspen Lake. A hometown boy! Y'all know his dad, Jesse. One of the Cariboo's finest tie-down ropers…. Seventy-one. That's the score Cody's gotta beat. Okay, he's sliding up on that rope now…making a last adjustment. Let's see what he can do."

The gate flies open and the steer blasts into the arena. For a split second, it glares at the crowd. Then with a wicked twist, it drops its head and kicks its back legs straight up, snapping Cody into a whiplash. He's hanging onto the strap with one hand, his other hand raised up above his shoulder. He sweeps his legs forward. He's almost lying flat on the steer's back.

One, two, three.

He's flung forward, then snapped back and forth like a rag.

Six, seven, eight.

The buzzer rings but Cody's still hanging on. The steer gives one last twist, and he flies off.

There's so much clapping I can hardly hear the announcer. "A qualifying round for our young cowboy here. Don't go away and we'll get that score for you."

Cody stands up, brushes off his legs and picks up his hat. He walks across the sand. He looks up at the bleachers, right where we're sitting.

"Way to go, Cody!" someone shouts. A girl, two rows below. She smooths her long, loose black hair and turns to someone beside her, and I can see that she's First Nations.

Cody waves at her.

"Seventy-three for Cody Cooper! That's a new high for our junior steer riders right here at Aspen Lake. Remember that name, folks. Looks like we've got ourselves a champion."

~

"They always save the barrel racing to the end," says Amber. "That's because everyone loves it. It'll take a while to set up. They'll want to rake the sand really smooth first."

"Then I'm going for a walk," I say.

I step down the bleacher and wander past the concession stand and the beer garden to the chutes at the end of the arena. There's a big, long barn, wide open at the front. A man wearing a black cowboy hat and chaps is leading a smoky gray horse out, its hooves clattering on the cement. I dodge out of the way, then peer inside.

Along both sides, horses are hanging their heads over stall doors. Am I allowed in here? I take a chance and go in. After the bright sun, it's dim and way cooler. I walk right through to the end of the barn, admiring all the horses and breathing in the smell, which I think is hay and horses and leather all mixed together. It smells like Margaret's barn but stronger. I love it.

Back outside, more horses are standing in enclosures made of metal pipes along one side of the barn. A girl in faded jeans and a turquoise tank top is grooming a brown horse with a black mane and tail. A cowboy who's leaning against the enclosure says something and they both laugh.

This is the side of the rodeo that people in the bleachers don't see. What would it be like to be part of it?

I'm thinking I should go back but then I see Cody. He's talking to a cowboy who's standing beside a black horse that keeps whinnying. The cowboy swings up into the saddle and the horse trots off, tail swishing.

I walk over. "Hey, Cody."

"Oh, hey Rachel. I saw you sitting with Amber. What do you think?"

"It's amazing."

He grins.

"And congratulations on winning the steer riding."

"Thanks. It was a good ride. I got lucky. You staying for the barrel racing?"

"Yeah."

"Good. I just gotta check on one of our horses and then I'll come sit with you."

CHAPTER THIRTY

When I get back to the bleachers, two men are rolling three big barrels with blue and white stripes into the arena. They space them apart at the points of a triangle.

I check the program. Fourteen entries. All girls.

"Okay folks, first off is Kirsten Wade from Ashcroft. She's riding Blue Moon, a real pretty quarter horse."

Amber starts a running commentary about clover leaf patterns, the sixty-second time limit, proper technique, flying changes, tight turns. I don't pay much attention. It's boiling hot and I've scorched my shoulders and I don't think Cody's coming.

Then a girl on a black horse blows into the arena. A man drops a red flag. She streaks around the barrels, leaning sideways at each turn. It's over before I can figure out what happened. It's amazing.

"Twenty-five seconds," says Amber. "Great ride."

The sixth rider goes so fast she misses a barrel.

"Disqualified," says Amber.

Cody leaps up the bleachers. "Shove over," he says to Jane, tapping the top of her head. He plunks down beside me.

"How ya doing, Amber?" he says.

"Hey, Cody. I'm good."

The eleventh rider hits a barrel and sends it flying.

"Time penalty," says Amber. "She's toast."

"Man, they're really burning around those barrels," says Cody.

"You're not kidding," I say.

There's a little break. Amber passes Cody a coke from the cooler. Jane's staring at him, and I give her the evil eye. I don't need one of her boyfriend comments right now.

"Okay, folks, number thirteen is our own Carlee Sparrow riding Copper Strike."

"Yo, Carlee!" shouts Cody.

The crowd stamps their feet. The man in front of me gives an ear-splitting whistle. Ten seconds later, a girl pounds into the arena on a wiry brown horse.

Cody leans forward, his hands on his knees.

Her white cowboy hat is airborne, her thick black braid flying out behind her. Her long legs are clamped to her horse's sides.

Copper Strike hugs the first barrel so tight I think for sure they're going to crash into it. As they round the second barrel, his shoulder almost touches the ground. He hangs there, suspended. Carlee throws her body the other way, but it's too late. Copper Strike skids out and crashes to the ground, rolls, and Carlee is flung off.

"Shit!" says Cody. The crowd has stopped breathing. I've stopped breathing. Jane's mouth is hanging open. Even Amber has shut up.

Carlee's up. Copper Strike scrabbles to his feet. Carlee runs up to him and grabs the reins.

Cody jumps up. "I gotta get down there. Good seeing you, Rachel. I'll see you around."

"Yeah. See you."

He jumps to the ground from the third bleacher. Then I look back at Carlee, who's stroking Copper Strike's neck and talking to him while she leads him slowly out of the arena.

"That is *so* Carlee," says Amber. "She adores all her horses. She reminds me so much of your mom."

"Mom?"

"Yeah. Barrel racing was her big event. Her and Magic. They were stars. Cleaned up on everything local. The work she put into him? Crazy! They were heading for the big time when she left."

Carlee's standing outside the fence holding Copper Strike's reins and talking to Cody. I can see her better now. She's the First Nations girl who was sitting in front of us. The girl Cody waved to. He laughs and gives her a big hug.

I don't care. All I can think about is Magic and Mom.

~

3 A.M.

"Wayne and I met at a rodeo," says Margaret. "In Clinton. He was a very handsome cowboy."

We're in the kitchen. I'm making the cocoa tonight.

"Amber said that Magic was a barrel racing horse."

"Yes, he was very talented. Your mom, too. She worked and worked with him. It was so hard to understand…." She rubs the skin beside her eyes. They're like dark smudges.

"Could Magic still do that? Barrel race?"

"No, his days for that are over. He's twenty-five. But he's still got lots of years left in him. He's a wonderful horse."

While I'm waiting for the milk to heat up, I think about last summer. Mom said she was taking us somewhere and it was a surprise and we couldn't ask her any questions. We had to wait for ages on Oak Street with our thumbs out until a guy in a black SUV finally stopped and picked us up.

I remember, after we left the city, looking out the window at the patches of farms and fields, stuck between the busy highway and gas stations and strip malls, and wondering what it would be like to live in the country.

We got dumped off at a sign on the road that said *Rocking Horse Stables*. Mom had booked an hour's ride for me and Jane. We were late and the woman who ran the place said we could have half an hour in her riding ring. Not enough time left for a trail ride.

Mom argued with her. I said I was going to pass. At the end, the woman stuck Jane on a very short, fat, white horse in the middle of this dusty riding ring and disappeared.

The horse ambled to the corner of the fence where there was some grass and started to eat.

"Pull his head up," said Mom.

"I can't," said Jane.

"Kick him. Don't let him do that. Make him walk."

"I can't."

"Jesus, Jane. This is costing good money. Pull the reins harder."

Jane started to wail.

Mom fumed all the way home. At Jane, for not trying harder. At the woman, for running a "dirty riding stable with horses that no one cared enough about to train."

At me, for laughing when Jane's horse wouldn't budge.

"You're a million miles away, Rachel," says Margaret now.

I pull myself back. "Amber said she would go riding with me. She wants to take me to Butterfly Lake. I'd like to go."

Margaret plays with a napkin left on the table from dinner.

"Is it far from here?" I say.

"Is what far from here?"

"Butterfly Lake."

Margaret's shredded the napkin into pieces. She pushes them aside.

"I imagine Amber's going to be far too busy to go riding with you," she says. "I have no idea what she's talking about. She prattles on about all kinds of things."

She stands up. "I think I'll skip the cocoa, but thank you, Rachel. We should both try to get some sleep."

She pauses at the door. "There's no lake around here called Butterfly Lake. Amber's just being fanciful. If there was, I would know."

~

Someone's lying. Amber, or Margaret?

CHAPTER THIRTY-ONE

I'm on the verandah, reading *The Shadow Soul* by Kaitlyn Davis. These library books are seriously overdue. I'm not opening texts or emails from the West End Library.

Margaret comes out and sits in the old armchair beside me. "I've got something for you," she says.

It's a yellow and white envelope.

She hands it to me. "These photos were in your Mom's old camera. I just found the camera a couple of months ago in a box of things from her room."

I'm staring at the *yellow and white envelope*. I almost shout, "Eureka! I've found it!"

But it doesn't make sense. Wayne said, *Don't tell Margaret.* And Margaret had it all along. I have no idea what's going on.

"It's all digital now," says Margaret. "But this camera used film. We weren't sure if you can even develop old film anymore, but Martin knows a place in Kamloops that still does. He and Wayne went down together. It was one of Wayne's good days."

She gets up. "You keep them."

I wait until she's gone then open the envelope. There's a stack of colored photos.

I rifle through them quickly, then go back and take my time. They're of Mom and Magic, barrel racing. They're streaking around the barrels, kicking up dust. In one, Mom's cowboy hat is in the air, her long hair flying behind her. There's an amazing close-up shot—Mom biting down on her lower lip, Magic's shoulder almost touching the ground. Even more impressive than Carlee and Copper Strike.

I search the photos for details—Mom's cowboy hat is black, and she has tan leather chaps over her jeans. She's wearing a long-sleeved red shirt trimmed with black braid and a white bandana. Her cowboy boots…. I look closely…they're dark red. She's wearing my boots.

They were stars. Cleaning up on everything. Heading for the big time.

I take a deep breath and try to center myself, the way Aura and I practiced. I look at the last two photos at the bottom of the stack. A golden retriever that's bigger than Bella lying on the verandah. An orange and black butterfly on a yellow flower. I recognize the fence. It's Margaret's garden.

Then I go back to the photos of Mom.

Finally, I put them all back and read the front of the envelope.

There are headings with boxes to tick off.

SETS:
1 set 2 sets (1 set checked)

EXPOSURES:
8 12 15 24 25 27 36 40 (12 checked)

FILM TYPE:
Color black and white (color checked)

PRICE:
Prints made: 12
Total: $4.50

For a few seconds, I absorb that information. *Prints made: 12.* I slide all the photos out again and count them. Eleven. One photo is missing.

~

I'm sitting on the grass in the sun. Margaret gave me a small round tin of saddle soap. I rub the pale yellow cream into the worn cracks and folds of my cowboy boots. Our cowboy boots. I keep polishing until all the dust and dirt has disappeared and the red leather gleams.

CHAPTER THIRTY-TWO

Jane and Wayne are sorting bones on the verandah. I'm washing the lunch dishes, and Margaret's making mountains of peanut butter cookies.

"Last batch," she says, sliding a cookie sheet into the oven. "How about you and I go for a ride when you're done? Just the two of us."

"No thank—"

What do I really want to do?

"Yes, I'd love that," I say.

~

We ride past the old homestead and onto a new trail that winds through a forest where all the trees have white trunks. It's beautiful.

"This is the Woodpecker Trail," says Margaret. She points out all the small round holes in the trunks of the trees.

The trail dips up and down and sometimes the horses have to step over fallen logs. We pass some huge boulders that Margaret says date from the Ice Age. Then we ride through an area where moss covers everything in an emerald green carpet.

Magic is brilliant. I love how he sways when he walks. I love leaning forward and patting his neck so his ears swivel back toward me as if he's saying, "I know you're there."

The trail widens and we can ride side by side.

"Magic is a quarter horse," says Margaret. "He was born on this ranch. He was a very gangly little foal. He'd topple right over when he tried to run. But your mom fell in love with him. She was only nine. She thought of the name Magic. Wayne helped her train him."

I'm listening and I'm trying so hard to picture all this and I can't. I just can't.

"Are you up for trying a trot?" says Margaret.

"I think so."

"We'll go in front, and you and Magic can stay behind us. Magic will copy Dancer. You don't have to do anything. Just relax."

Dancer breaks into a trot and suddenly Magic's trotting, too. It's way faster than I'm expecting and it's choppy. I grab the horn. I'm bouncing up and down, banging against the saddle, and then my right foot slides out of the stirrup and I tumble forward on Magic's neck.

I holler, "Whoa!" and Margaret glances back and everything slows down again and I catch my breath.

"You okay?"

"I think so."

"We'll do another trot up by that pine tree. Sink your heels down and melt into the saddle."

"Okay."

"Ready?"

"Ready."

I'm slamming against the saddle. *Bang! Bang! Bang!* Magic must hate me. And then, for exactly eight seconds (forever), I'm melting.

We slow to a walk and Margaret says, "That was much better."

I blow out a big breath of air. "Can we do it again?"

~

There's a commercial on TV where this woman staggers out of her house and raises a flag on a pole on her front lawn. The flag says, "I SLEPT."

That's me this morning.

I SLEPT.

~

I put a pot of tea, a cup, and a plate of toast on a tray and bring it to Margaret's room. The curtains are pulled.

I hesitate in the doorway. "Thank you, Rachel," she murmurs.

"Is your head really bad?"

"Not too bad."

"I've brought you some tea and toast."

"That's lovely. Set it over there on the dresser. I'm going to try to get up soon."

There's enough light from the hallway for me to see a long dark dresser with a huge oval mirror above it. It's covered with photos in small frames. I set the tray down and pick up one of the frames. It's a little girl, smiling, with a gap between her front teeth.

"Wayne can't look at pictures of the kids," says Margaret.

I turn around, still holding the photo of Mom. I know it's Mom because her pigtails are bright red.

"Why not?"

"It just upsets him. Makes him sad. We used to have so many pictures of the kids in the living room. But now they're all here."

I notice then that there are framed photos on the wall, too, bigger ones. Faces of children and teenagers, shadowy in the dark room.

"When I'm feeling better," says Margaret, "we'll look at them together."

~

"There's something under here." Jane's on her hands and knees, peering under our bunk bed.

"It's nothing."

"It's a laptop." She pulls it out.

"Okay, it's a laptop. But it's not yours."

"Where did you get it?"

"I found it."

"Why are you hiding it?"

"You've got five seconds to scram. One, two, three—"

"But why—?"

"—four, five."

When she's gone, I push the button on the side of the laptop and the little drawer slides out. I pick up the CD. I could see if it would work in one of the school computers. But I really don't want to do that.

The yurt, summer 2005. I think Mom was still living here then. If I ever get a chance to watch this CD, I need to be by myself.

~

Jane's reading in the hammock. It's a stretchy, stringy hammock and she's wrapped inside like she's in a cocoon. I can just see the edge of a book and a long golden tail.

The hammock is strategically located near the edge of the mowed grass, right by the woods. I sneak through the trees like a panther, drop to my knees, and crawl across five meters of no-man's land. I position myself under the hammock.

"WHOOOHOWHOOOHOOHOO...."

Jane leans over the side and smacks me on my head with her book.

"I'M RIIIIISING FROM THE DEEEEP...."

I hunch my back and shoulders and stand up. Jane flies out one side. Bella flies out the other side. I laugh so hard I pee my jeans. And that makes Jane laugh even harder than me.

CHAPTER THIRTY-THREE

I've tied Magic to the hitching post while I tug a comb through some tangles in his thick, black mane. He's looking way shinier since I've been taking care of him. Margaret's going to pick up some special supplements in Hundred Mile so I can make him a hot bran mash at night.

Amber's car lumbers down the driveway; she's dropping Jane off. They both hop out of the car.

"See you!" says Amber, as Jane scampers away.

She walks over and pats Magic's neck. "I still want to get out for a ride with you, Rachel. I've just been mega busy."

I'm okay with Amber now. She was fun at the rodeo and Jane loves her. "That's okay."

"Margaret around?"

She's in the garden picking beans, but I have my loyalties. "She's lying down," I say.

"Those headaches are a plague. I won't disturb her then," says Amber. "Hey, how's your Uncle Rob doing?"

"He's fine. Why?"

"Oh, I don't know. I was just wondering. I used to have the worst crush on him. Maybe because he's older, he always seemed so attractive."

A little pause. "I hear he's back in Canada. And he's married."

"Yup. To Aleksandra. She's Polish."

Amber sighs. "Nice?"

"She's okay."

"Are they going back to Poland?"

"Dunno." It's a lifetime ago that I found that letter from the Warsaw Hospital in the printer.

I drop the comb in the grooming kit and untie the lead rope. "I'm taking Magic back to the field now," I say.

"I'll walk with you." Magic whinnies when I slip off his halter and he trots over to Dixie and Dancer. We lean against the fence as the horses graze.

"Mom said he's been coming up for weekends a lot."

Uncle Rob again. "He was. He's pretty busy right now but he's going to try to come up soon."

"That's nice for Margaret. I don't know what Wayne thinks about it."

"Why?"

"Oh, he and Rob clashed so much. Wayne was always losing his temper with him. He's so controlling, that's his problem. He's the reason Rob left as soon as he could. Jimmy stuck it out because he wanted the ranch. This fifth or sixth generation

Bird thing. I call it the Bird curse. My mom says she doesn't know how Margaret put up with it all these years. Wayne never stops talking about the amazing Birds who came from Alabama or God knows where and built this place in the wilderness with their bare hands! Blah, blah, blah. Jimmy was into it, too."

I laugh. "Texas."

She laughs, too. "I shouldn't be bad-mouthing Wayne. He *is* your grandfather. How are you getting along with him?"

"Okay. Jane sticks to him like glue."

"Yeah, well, he always was better with girls."

"How did Uncle Jimmy die?" I say then. "I know it was an accident with his hunting rifle, but I don't know what happened exactly."

Amber looks surprised. And wary. "No one's told you?"

"No. No one talks about it."

But there are all those guns in the yurt.

Amber's face has turned pale under her freckles. She steps into her car and turns on the engine. She starts to roll up her window, then says, "It's Margaret you should ask, not me."

CHAPTER THIRTY-FOUR

I'm sorting out the recycling for Margaret. She's the organized one in this house. There are two bins each for plastics and tin cans, two for cardboard, and three for paper. She's been going through cupboards, tossing out years of accumulated stuff.

She asked me to make sure there's no toilet paper rolls mixed in with the paper. You can get in major trouble for that in Hundred Mile.

I dump out the bin. Grocery store flyers, catalogues, knitting patterns, telephone bills, hydro bills, and recipes torn out of magazines slide all over the floor. No toilet paper rolls but a great big evil paper towel roll, which is probably worse. I toss it in the cardboard bin.

I pick up some pages held together with a paper clip (paper clip into the tin can bin). There's a heading on the top page: *Amber Gordon Vacation Land Realtors, 100 Mile House, BC.*

I glance through the rest. There's lots of stuff about lot numbers and grazing licenses. I'm not sure but it looks like it might be some kind of listing agreement for the ranch.

Did Margaret mean to throw this away? Wayne doesn't want to sell. I'm beginning to think that Margaret doesn't really want to either. You'd expect her to be sad. This place must be full of memories. But it's the way she looks sometimes. Like she's *afraid* to sell the ranch. Afraid to move somewhere new? Afraid of something else?

Does Amber know?

I bury the papers deep in the bottom of the bin.

~

Sometimes Margaret goes riding early in the morning by herself. She's fixing fences.

She and Wayne are arguing about it on the verandah. I'm reading *The Shadow Queen* and, at the same time, stressing about how to get my library books back to the library in Vancouver before I owe a zillion dollars in overdue fines. Jane's sorting her bone collection, which has grown to include a headless rabbit skeleton (who ate its head???), a coyote's backbone, a weasel's rib, and lots of cow legs. She keeps dragging them back from rides, tied to our saddles, and Wayne keeps identifying them. Her dream is to find moose antlers and a skull (cow) like the one over the barn door.

They're arguing because Margaret thinks the ranch is falling apart. I'm guessing Wayne feels shitty that he can't do the work.

"It was different before," says Margaret. "It's too much now."

Wayne smashes his hand on the table and shouts, "We're not selling."

Jane hates it when Wayne yells.

"Let's take Bella for a walk," I say quickly.

When we get back, Wayne's in his room and Margaret's in her garden.

~

This afternoon, we're all riding—me, Margaret, and Jane—on what Margaret calls the Bear Trail. It's shady and it follows an old fence with rusty wire stretched between posts.

"Keep your eyes open for rocks flipped over. Like that one there." Margaret points to a rock lying beside a hole in the ground. "An old bear comes along here most days turning over rocks to look for ants."

Too much information. This is not a good time to think about the bear that tried to destroy the verandah.

When we come to places where the wire is pulled down, Margaret stops Dancer and says, "Hang on a minute," gets off, and drops the reins. She keeps brown leather gloves, something called fencing pliers, thick staples, and a roll of wire in her saddlebag. Sometimes I get down, too, and hold the wire while she staples it to the post.

It's barbed wire. "Be very careful," says Margaret. She shows me a long, jagged tear in the thumb of one of her gloves. "Even with these heavy gloves, barbed wire is nasty."

When the wire is broken, she twists each end into a loop, attaches a new piece of wire in between, and yanks it tight.

We dip down into a shallow gully and you can glimpse the marsh through the trees. A horrible stench wafts over.

"EEEEWWW!" says Jane. "What's that?"

"A moose carcass," says Margaret. "I spotted it the other day. It's just down that slope. I think wolves killed it."

Jane lights up. "Antlers!"

"No," says Margaret firmly. "It's a fresh kill and fresh kills attract bears. We're steering clear."

"Unfair!" says Jane.

Great. She's turned into a turkey vulture.

"We'll come back in a few weeks," says Margaret. "When the bones are picked clean."

CHAPTER THIRTY-FIVE

I'm leaning back in the chair with my feet on Wayne's desk. Reading. It's hard going. His handwriting is almost illegible.

The *thud thud* of his canes comes from the hallway. Wayne glowers at me from the doorway. I drop my feet and sit up, waving the stack of papers in my hand. "Is this true?" I say.

"Give me that," he says.

I hand over the papers, and he skims over the top page and turns to the next one.

"Daryl and Daphne Bird stayed the whole winter in a cabin that was three meters long and two meters wide?" I say. "In fifty below? During blizzards? Just so they could feed some cows?"

"Cows, girlie, are what your great-great-grandfather founded this family on. He drove a herd of purebred, longhorn Scottish cattle all the way from Texas to Saskatchewan and then across the Rockies. Of course it's true. And it was a hard life.

Sweltering heat in the prairies. Dust storms that blinded you. But the winters were worse. Four feet of snow in one night. Ice storms that snapped massive trees like they were twigs."

"That's brutal," I say.

"You don't know the half of it. You've been living a soft city life. The Birds are tough stock. When my father, Joseph Bird, was thirteen, he had to ride on horseback through snow drifts over his head, carrying blocks of frozen milk from the home ranch to the cow cabins. Do you think I'm making this stuff up?"

"No, but maybe exaggerating."

"You have a look at this."

He thumps over to a big map pinned to the wall. "This is the Double D Ranch."

I walk over and follow his finger as he points out Aspen Lake, the old homestead, the "new" house, the marsh, the hay-fields, the hay shed. He jabs a spot somewhere to the right of the homestead where there's a tiny black square.

"That's one of Daryl and Daphne Bird's cow cabins. The only one left. They built it before the homestead, over a hundred years ago. You take Jane and see if you can find it. The last time I was there was ten years ago, and the old cabin was disappearing fast. You'll have to look hard, which is not something you're good at."

Nice shot.

"You need to be more organized, which is not something you're good at," I say.

"Maybe I took the photo out of the envelope," he says.

So it *is* just one photo that he's looking for. Should I tell him that Margaret had the envelope of photos and that she gave it to me? Margaret's not supposed to know about this. *Don't tell Margaret.*

"It would help if I knew what it was a photo of," I say.

"I'm tired," he says. "You can look later. Go on. Get out of here."

~

We've been thrashing around for an hour, tripping over the broken-down snake fence, stepping into gopher holes hidden in the grass. We keep going back to the old homestead and starting again.

The grass, weeds, and nettles are waist high. Jane gives up looking and plunks down in the middle of the grass to scratch her mosquito bites. I turn around and she's gone.

Then she pops up and says, "Is this what we're looking for?"

It's a piece of rusty stove pipe, about fifteen meters away. Jane has eagle eyes. She's found Daryl and Daphne Bird's cow cabin.

We pull back weeds, grass, and nettles, uncovering another piece of the stove pipe and chunks of old, rotten logs sunk into the ground. They're laid out in a rough rectangle. A few old logs, still standing, look like part of a wall. I pace it out. Wayne was right. It's about three meters long and two meters wide. Jane finds some rough broken boards nailed together that could be an old door.

We lie on our backs in the grass inside the rectangle of logs, side by side, gazing up at the blue sky.

"What would it have been like to live here?" I say to Jane.

"Where did they pee?" she asks.

"In a bucket."

"Yuck. Where did they put their food?"

"Beside the stove."

"Then where did they put their dishes?" she says.

"They just had one big pot and a tin plate and a fork and a knife each. They put them beside their feet."

"Where did they put their clothes?"

"Beside their heads."

"Where did they put their books?"

"Didn't have any."

"Was it fun?"

"Are you kidding me? Super fun. Now Daphne, you get up and make us some nice squirrel stew while I have a nap. And please go outside in this raging blizzard and chop some firewood."

"Then you have to go and kill a bear," says Jane, "and we lost our gun, so you have to do it with your bare hands."

"I'm on it, Daphne."

"Me too."

"We're good at this," I say. "In our next lives, we'll be pioneers."

"Go and get some berries," orders Jane.

"I've got an idea," I say. "Let's lie here and see how still we can be."

I close my eyes. I love it when it snows in Vancouver. I love how everything becomes quiet and beautiful. But it hardly ever snows there, and it doesn't stay beautiful long. The cars turn it to brown slush and then it rains.

Here, it snows a meter and a half overnight. I'm picturing Daphne digging her way out through her low doorway. The tiny cabin is buried in snow. The marsh is covered in a blanket of pure white.

She's got all her pioneer chores to do. Instead, she makes a snow angel.

CHAPTER THIRTY-SIX

Bella's scratching the mudroom door. We're in the middle of dinner. Margaret's meatloaf, mashed potatoes, and green beans from the garden.

"I'll let her in!" says Jane, leaping up.

There's a mournful howl. Jane calls out, "She smells funny."

Bella skulks into the kitchen with Jane behind her, holding her nose.

"EEWWWW," Margaret and I say at the same time.

"What is it?" says Jane.

"She's been skunked," says Wayne.

~

HOW TO DESKUNK A DOG:

1. Bathe your dog in dog shampoo.
2. Dry her off then cover her in tomato juice, saturating the coat completely.
3. Let the juice soak in for ten to twenty minutes before rinsing it out.
4. Wash your dog again with dog shampoo.

~

It doesn't work. Jane and Bella smell like skunk and tomato juice. I'm watching from afar. I'm having no part of this. Susan brings over a bottle of *SKUNK OFF*, which is a special shampoo just for this problem. It's lavender scented and very sudsy. Bella has four baths.

Now Jane and Bella smell like skunk and lavender perfume. Apparently it will wear off. Bella's going to stay outside for a year or two. Jane's in the tub upstairs having a coconut bubble bath.

~

We're beside the fence line at the bottom corner of a gently sloping field.

"This is a good place," says Margaret. "We don't have to worry about the horses stepping into gopher holes here. And it's always easier going uphill. They won't get going too fast."

In a split second, she and Dancer take off.

I grab the saddle horn and then I let go because this is so

different from trotting. It's smooth, like a rocking chair. My hips are moving with Magic. Melting.

He's falling behind so I squeeze my legs. He picks up speed. We're in a sea of tall waving grass and my braids are bouncing and I can't see anything but I'm good.

And now, finally, I can picture Mom and Magic and I can't stop smiling.

My first lope.

CHAPTER THIRTY-SEVEN

"Cody called when you were feeding the horses," says Margaret. She's at the kitchen sink, attacking a pan crusted with dried meatloaf from last night. She doesn't turn around.

"Cody Cooper?"

"That's the only Cody I know in Aspen Lake."

"Did he say what he wanted?"

She turns around, still holding the pan. She keeps it from dripping on the floor with the dishrag. "He wants to know if you want to go waterskiing on Sunday. He and his friends are getting together over at the Vandermeyer's place. I wrote his number down on that pad of paper by the phone."

I don't waterski. Correction: I've never *tried* waterskiing. I think of how Aura said I automatically say no before stopping to think what I really want.

What I really want is to see Cody again.

"So, I can tell him yes?"

"It's up to you."

I try to read her face. Something's wrong. What is it about Cody that she doesn't like?

"I think I'll go then. Will you drive me?"

Margaret nods and turns back to her pan.

~

I'm not surprised when Margaret drops me off at the end of the Vandermeyer's driveway. She's not into making small talk with anyone. I've got my backpack with a towel, sunscreen, and my water bottle. I'm wearing a T-shirt over my new one-piece turquoise bathing suit. It's high cut on my thighs and I feel good in it. Flip-flops. I'm ready.

Jane waves good-bye from the open trunk window. Margaret's taking her to the store for ice cream. I wave back and set off.

The driveway winds through trees and ends in a big open space at a log house with a blue metal roof. Just past it is the lake. I don't see anyone, but I hear people talking and laughing. I walk around the house and look across a lawn to the lake. A bunch of kids are standing and sitting on a long dock and there's a big boat at the end.

Cody's leaning out the back of the boat talking to a girl sitting on the edge of the dock. It's Carlee Sparrow, holding on to a handle attached to a line. One of the guys on the dock calls out something and Cody turns his head. He sees me and shouts, "Hey, Rachel! Come on! Get in!"

Can you screw up getting into a boat? I lower one leg over the side, my foot touches the deck and I swing my other foot over. The boat rocks. I slide onto a green vinyl seat.

There's a girl with dark cropped hair at the wheel, wearing an orange bikini. Carlee's in a bright red one-piece like me. Cody's in long, baggy swim shorts.

"This is Rachel," he says. "Carlee. Sarah."

They both say hi, then Sarah guns the engine. The bow of the boat tips up, the line goes taut, and Carlee stands up, so smooth, both feet on one ski.

"Slalom," says Cody. He's guessed I know nothing. "She gets up on one ski every time. I have to start on two and drop one."

I saw Carlee barrel race. One look and you know she's going to be a pro at this, too.

She makes it look easy, streaking back and forth, crossing the wake and skimming across the smooth water. She tilts her body until she's almost horizontal, like she did on Copper Strike. Her ski sends an arc of water high into the air.

"Carlee likes a wild ride," says Cody. "Come on, Sarah. Give it to her."

No matter what Sarah throws at her, Carlee stays up. Finally, she raises her hand, Sarah cuts the engine, and Carlee sinks into the lake. She's laughing when Cody helps pull her up into the boat.

"You want to try, Rachel?" says Cody.

I *did*, but I don't anymore. I shake my head. "No thanks."

Sarah cruises back to the dock. People switch places. Someone called Matt is driving, Tyson is skiing. Carlee bends over from the waist and shakes her long black hair. "I'll spot," she says.

Cody introduces me to everyone. Zero chance I can remember all these names.

I'm trying to figure out if Cody and Carlee are a couple.

A girl (Makayla?) wearing a microscopic purple bikini points to an open cooler with cans floating in ice cubes. "Help yourself."

Everyone's holding something so I grab a coke. I get a lot of "How do you like Aspen Lake?" questions.

"It's great," I say. "I love it here."

Then the waterskiing ends. I talk to Carlee for a while about the rodeo. I tell her about Magic, and she's interested. She's actually really nice. Someone brings out a big orange tube. A competition starts on who can dump the person on the tube the fastest. Every time the boat comes back to the dock, there's more switching places.

It's my turn. I'm in the back of the boat, Cody's driving, and Carlee's sliding the tube into the water. I'm the official spotter.

Cody dumps Carlee in thirty seconds.

"Jerk!" she yells, treading water beside the tube. She climbs back into the boat. "Your turn, Rachel. I'll spot."

I can do this.

A minute later, I'm on.

"Grab the handles," says Carlee. "Hold on tight."

I grip the handles so hard my fingers hurt.

"Be nice, Cody," she says.

The rope flies out. It's tight. "Ready?" shouts Cody.

I shut my eyes and hold up my thumb.

We're moving but it's super slow. I stick up my thumb again and the tube jerks and suddenly I'm crashing up and down in the wake. I'm hanging on with a death-grip now. How do I steer this thing? How do I get out of the wake?

Two more enormous bounces and I'm hydroplaning over the water, and it's amazing and now I can open my eyes. A few more seconds of glorious flying and crash, back across the wake. I'm picking up speed big-time.

Everything happens after that at warp speed. A boat is heading straight for me, its bow up in the air. It's going to mow me down. Carlee's shouting, waving her arms, dancing up and down. At the very last second, the boat veers away in a wide arc. I hit a huge swell. The tube flies into the air and I think Cody cuts the engine, but I don't know for sure because the tube flips on its side at a hundred miles an hour and buries me in the lake.

I come up spluttering and gasping for air. My nose is on fire from all the water that got shoved up it. I tread water while Cody circles the boat and coasts in beside me.

"You okay, Rachel?" says Carlee.

"Yes," I gasp.

"Idiot driver," says Cody. "What a moron. He wasn't even looking. But hey, that was an impressive wipeout. What do you want to do? You gettin' out?"

I push my wet hair out of my eyes. "Not yet."

~

PLAN G: STAY HERE FOREVER.

~

Cody says his dad, Jesse, is picking him up. He can drop me off at the store and save Margaret part of the drive. I use Uncle Rob's secret code to call her. Ring. Hang up. Count to fifteen. Dial and let it ring again. She says she'll meet me at the store. As she hangs up, she says, "No more ice cream today, Jane."

Jesse drives a big brown pickup. I sit in the front between him and Cody. I'm damp, hot, burnt, but I feel good.

"Nice to meet you, Rachel," says Jesse. "I knew your mom and your Uncle Jimmy really well. Man, you look just like Layla. I'm real sorry for your loss."

"Yeah, well, thanks," I say.

Jesse's wearing a sleeveless white T-shirt. He has a very cool tattoo on his shoulder.

"Nice tattoo," I say. "It's a Viking compass, right?"

He turns and grins at me. "Right. How did you know that?"

"I was looking at a Norse mythology site."

"You're interested in stuff like that?"

"Yup."

"See Cody? Cool people are into Norse mythology."

Cody groans.

A blue pickup passes, going the opposite direction, and the driver and Jesse both honk.

"So, Rachel," says Jesse. "I hear you went to the rodeo. What did you think?"

"I loved it."

"Cody did good, eh?"

"That's for sure."

"I just scraped into the junior category this year," says Cody. "My birthday's at the end of this month, then I'll be sixteen."

Bells are ringing. He's eleven months older than me. He'll be going into grade eleven.

"You'll be riding steers with the big guys next year," says Jesse. "Bring you down a notch."

When we get to the store, Margaret's not there. I knew she wouldn't be.

"Thanks very much for the ride," I say. "I'm fine. You don't have to wait. And thanks for asking me, Cody."

"I'll text you."

I sit on the bench in front of the store and dig into my backpack. My unopened can of coke has probably steeped to some kind of toxic tea by now. I leave it on the bench and take out my water bottle.

Margaret will be a while. She won't get here until she is sure that Jesse and Cody have gone. It's weird. I like Margaret. She gets Jane. Everybody seems happy when they see her. But she's so unfriendly. Why?

I had a good day. Next time, I'm waterskiing.

~

CODY: How's your sunburn?

ME: Red.

~

ME: If you wanted to hide the password for your laptop, where would you put it?

JASON: I'd keep it in my head.

ME: That's a big help.

JASON: Lots of people put it on the bottom of the laptop.

~

I turn the laptop over.
      Black felt pen on a piece of masking tape.

LAyLA

CHAPTER THIRTY-EIGHT

I'm in Mom's old bedroom. I've brought the CD and Uncle Jimmy's laptop.

In the end, coming in here was no big deal. Whatever I was scared about, it didn't happen. Maybe it's something to do with that *you can't leave a place you've never been to* thing. Letting yourself feel all the stuff that's happened before you move on. Jason's new mantra. Am I moving on? I don't know.

But I did it. I opened the door to Mom's old bedroom and I came inside and nothing bad happened to me. It's just a room.

It also might be because there's only one thing in here that reminds me of Mom and that's the poster on the wall opposite the bed. That's all. Everything else could belong to anyone—a blue dresser, a small, round night table with a lamp on it, a tall mirror on the inside of the door, a double bed covered with a brown and white quilt, a little desk. There's nothing in the drawers, nothing in the closet. I looked.

I knew right away that Mom put that poster there because it's an Amnesty International poster. There's a silhouette of a person balancing on one leg on top of a pyramid made out of rows and rows of words. Words written in bold, black letters. Words with no spaces between them.

DISCRIMINATIONEDUCATIONPRISONRACISM...

I look for a socket to plug the laptop in. I find one behind the night table. The screen lights up with JIMMY BIRD and the box for the password. I type LAYLA. The screen changes to a waterfall cascading down a mountain.

My heart's beating faster. I slide the CD into the drawer and close it. Then I wait.

The laptop whirrs and hums and I just know it's not going to work and then suddenly I'm watching a boy sawing a piece of wood on a sawhorse.

No sound.

He's in faded jeans. Bare feet. He stops and grins at the camera and waves. There's a tattoo on his shoulder. I pause the CD. The Viking compass. It's Jesse.

Still no sound.

Next, almost a whole minute of different angles of the yurt's floor which is half-made. Shots of the lake and the orange canoe and a golden retriever that looks a lot like Bella.

The person filming has got the hang of it or else someone else has taken over because the video's steady now. A girl wearing a tight blue T-shirt poses for the camera, turning sideways and pulling up her shirt to show off her stomach. She's pregnant. Really pregnant. Like the baby could be born at any minute. She has short, curly blonde hair and very long legs. She's so pretty.

There's a big click and a voice says, "Okay, we got sound."

Jesse and the pregnant girl are hugging. A long hug right over top of the bulging baby. Someone whistles.

A girl's voice calls out, "Slow down, Steph. You don't want the baby today!"

Steph. Stephanie. She's *pregnant*.

Amber's smiling into the camera. She's got all her freckles but she's way thinner and her hair is long. She's wearing a green tank top and a long, green, wraparound skirt. She does a little dance.

The camera moves to a boy in cut-off jeans, no shirt, with some kind of pendant around his neck. He looks so familiar, but I can't say exactly how.

Rewind.

My chest tightens. He looks like Mom.

Of course they were close. They were twins.

It's Uncle Jimmy.

Then Mom fills the screen. I feel a jolt, right in my gut. She looks so young. Her long red hair's in two braids and she's wearing a yellow bikini that I can't imagine her ever buying. She smiles. I've never seen my mom smile like that. Never. She looks radiant.

She turns away from the camera and it's her sunburnt shoulders that make me cry.

I stop the CD.

~

Stephanie was pregnant. She's with Jesse. The date written on the CD is summer 2005.

Sixteen years ago. Cody's birthday's at the end of July. He said he'll be sixteen. That means Stephanie is Cody's mother. She has to be.

Somehow, I had the feeling that it was just Cody and Jesse. But maybe I'm wrong. Maybe Cody lives with his dad and his mom.

Or maybe Stephanie's gone.

~

ME: Your mom and my mom were best friends.

CODY: I know.

ME: Why didn't you tell me?

CODY: I didn't think you'd want to talk about it.

ME: I do.

CODY: I'll bike over after work.

~

There's a rock on the bottom of the lake, about five meters from shore. It's flat like a table, a pale gray shadow under the water that we swim over. It's a monster, I tell Jane, lurking in its watery den. Sometimes we stand on it and jump. Today, for the first time, the top of the rock is above the surface. It's circled with white lines. Water marks.

Jane's been swimming underwater looking for dragonfly nymphs. I tap her shoulder. "Come on. Let's swim out to the rock."

It's baked by the sun, and we splash water on it before we sit down.

"Put your legs out to the side like this," I say, demonstrating.

We tilt our heads back so our wet hair falls like curtains of seaweed.

"In our next life," I say, "we'll be mermaids."

~

We're having lunch on the verandah. Cold chicken legs and potato salad. Jane and I are still in our bathing suits. We've just got back from the lake.

Wayne's having trouble with his fork. His hands are so swollen today. Margaret cuts his chicken into small pieces and he scowls, but he doesn't stop her.

Margaret picks up a napkin and fans herself. "It's strange that it's so humid," she says. "Strange for Aspen Lake."

"Weather's changing," grunts Wayne.

Jane's famished. She's talking with her mouth full. She takes a huge bite of her biscuit and starts into another story, this one about being mermaids on the rock.

"What rock?" says Margaret.

"It's in the lake," says Jane. "It's sticking out of the water, but it didn't do that before."

Margaret looks at Wayne.

"Why is it sticking out now?" says Jane.

"The level of the lake is dropping," says Wayne. "We need rain."

Margaret gets up and goes inside.

~

Margaret's not in her room. I've made iced tea and poured her a glass. I set it down on the night table and glance out the window. The garden gate is open. Margaret spends more and more time in the garden. She sits on an old twig chair by the raspberries for ages.

The blankets on the bed are messed and she's left three books by her pillow. Definitely a bad night. I know the signs. I pick up the books and put them on the night table. Then I straighten her blanket.

I find one more book. It has a pale blue leather cover with the word *Journal*. Aura suggested I keep a journal and I tried but it didn't work. I felt pressured to think of profound things to say and ended up just writing boring stuff about going to the library, going to the beach.

That was my life then.

For a while, I tried writing a list of the books I'd read. Now I don't even know where it is.

I wonder what Margaret writes about.

I pick up her journal to put it with the other books, and a piece of folded newspaper slides out the back.

I unfold it.

ASPEN LAKE WOMAN DIES IN HIT AND RUN

CHAPTER THIRTY-NINE

ASPEN LAKE WOMAN DIES IN HIT AND RUN

The woman who was struck down by a vehicle on Highway 24 on July 24 has been identified as Stephanie Robertson, 18 years old, of Aspen Lake. She was walking back to her home in the pull-off at the side of the highway, and was accompanied by a male, Jesse Cooper, 18 years old, also of Aspen Lake.

Robertson, eight and a half months pregnant, sustained multiple life-threatening injuries and was transported by ambulance to the Royal Inland Hospital in Kamloops. She died of her injuries on the morning of July 29, after giving birth to a baby boy. Simon Cooper, uncle of Jesse Cooper, the young man and father of the baby who was present at the accident, says the tight-knit community is grieving and that the family appreciates the outpouring of support.

Weather and driving conditions were likely a factor in the fatal accident. The police have no suspects but believe that someone in the community may have relevant information. They are urging them to contact the One Hundred Mile House RCMP.

I put the piece of newspaper back and leave the journal and the other books on the bed. I push the blanket to the bottom. I pick up the tray and leave. I don't know what I'm going to say to Cody.

When he gets here, we're just finishing dessert, raspberry crumble with ice cream, and I'm expecting Margaret will offer him some. She doesn't.

~

We sit on the bottom bunk, the laptop on a chair in front of us. Margaret said that the bedroom door has to stay open. She didn't say anything about the laptop. I don't think she even noticed it.

At the end, I just told Cody that I read the newspaper article and that I'm really sorry. He says that everyone in Aspen Lake knows what happened to his mom and he's okay with it.

He wants to see the CD.

I know what's coming, what to expect, and I'm still tensing up. Maybe Cody's seen lots of pictures of Stephanie but a video is different. I have no idea how he's going to react.

This time, I want to watch right to the end without looking away, without wanting to stop it.

Aura's coaching me silently. *Breathe.*

Cody slides the CD into the tray.

We don't say anything while the video plays. There's the part where Stephanie shows off her pregnant tummy and she and Jesse hug and maybe Cody's holding his breath because when the video moves to Amber doing her little dance he blows out air.

When we get to Mom in her yellow bikini and that incredible smile, I close my eyes for a second. *Breathe.* I watch the last two minutes.

Mom and Stephanie wade into the lake. They have a splashing fight. Jesse jumps in to join them. Stephanie slips, falls into the water. Jesse scoops her up. Then Mom soaks Jesse.

I glance sideways at Cody. He's leaning forward like he wants to be right there in the video with them.

The big golden retriever lunges out of the lake, shaking water on everyone. Amber yells, "Buster! Get away!"

Uncle Jimmy hoists up the end of a pole. The video is jerky again. A few seconds of Uncle Jimmy and the pole, then grass, then bushes, then blue sky. I'm guessing that's when Amber's filming.

Every time the camera points at Jesse, he gives a goofy wave.

"God, my dad was nerdy," says Cody. He seems okay but I have no clue what he's thinking inside.

Mom and Stephanie smile at the camera, their arms linked around each other, laughing.

Tears sting my eyes.

The screen goes black.

"You okay, Rachel?"

"Yeah. You?"

"Yeah, I'm good." He sighs. "Crazy, huh?"

"Yeah."

He pops the CD out. "*The yurt summer 2005*," he says. "The famous yurt. Dad says he can't understand why no one's torn it down."

"Tear it down? Why?" I say.

"Don't you know?"

"Know what?"

"Shit. I shouldn't have said anything."

"What?"

"I thought someone would've told you," he says. "That's where Jimmy shot himself."

"In the yurt? I thought it happened while he was hunting. Uncle Rob said it was an accident with his hunting rifle."

"It wasn't an accident." He hesitates. "It was suicide."

CHAPTER FORTY

We're inside the yurt.

Cody walks around and looks at everything. I unlock the cupboard to show him the guns.

"Six rifles," I say. "Don't you think that's freaky?"

Cody smiles. "They're not all rifles." He points. "Those two are. They're hunting rifles. He probably used them for hunting bears and deer. That one's a double-barrelled shotgun. It shoots shells full of pellets."

"What would that be for?"

"Birds. Ducks."

He picks up one of the guns. "This is a .22. It's good for target shooting. Maybe gophers."

"Oh." My picture of Uncle Jimmy shooting up a school is happily disappearing.

"Now this one's a beauty," says Cody. "It's a black powder rifle. From the old days."

"So where are all the bullets for these things?"

"Ammo," says Cody. "You never keep your ammo in the same place."

Right. Enough about guns. I close the cupboard and lock it.

Cody walks over to the bed and reads the Bible verses scrawled on the wall. "Now this *is* freaky. It's insane."

"So that's blood," I say, pointing to the brown dots sprayed over the words.

"Yeah, it must be."

"Then that's where he did it. On his bed." I feel like I'm going to vomit.

"He must have been so messed up," says Cody. "I wonder why?"

"Nobody talks about any of this stuff," I say. "Not even Uncle Rob. Or else they lie."

"What did he *do* in here?" says Cody. "There's no books, no movies. He had the laptop but there's no Wi-Fi, there's nothing."

"Just that Bible."

"Right. Searching the Bible for verses to make you feel like shit. Not my idea of a good time."

"There's one fork, one knife, one bowl, one mug," I say. "It's sad."

"Dad tried to reach out to Jimmy a few times," says Cody. "They used to be good friends. Dad came here once to see him. He said he thought he was having some mental health stuff going on. He was definitely drinking again. And then Margaret kept making it hard for Dad to visit. Dad said she made it clear she didn't want him interfering."

That's the Margaret I know. But why would she do that to Uncle Jimmy? What is she so afraid of?

"There's some binders in here," I say, opening one of the cupboards. "Cattle ranching stuff. I guess that's what he did every day. Read the Bible and read about cows."

Cody looks at the labels on the spines, then pulls out a thin red binder at the end of the row. It's filled with typed pages.

He scans the first page, flips to the next, reads a bit more.

"Take a look at this," he says. "Jimmy was really big into this sustainability issue."

I read Uncle Jimmy's notes out loud. "Thirty per cent of the world's land is used to raise livestock…. Cows cause over ten per cent of the world's greenhouse emissions…. Beef cattle need twenty-eight times more irrigation than pork, poultry, or dairy."

There's about twenty more pages of this.

Cody flips to the back of the binder and reads, "Action Plan for Aspen Lake Ranch. A range health assessment, identification of conservation areas, rotational grazing, assessment of nutritional and feed requirements to cut methane gas."

"That sounds like major work," I say.

"And big changes. Wayne would never have agreed to that. And it's not just Wayne. A lot of the ranchers think this way. They're old-timers. Raising cattle is a religion around here."

"Do you think raising cattle is bad?" I say.

"I don't know. My grandparents have a cattle ranch. That's all they know how to do. I've grown up with it."

This makes way more sense to Cody than to me. But I get it. Uncle Jimmy was worried about what cattle ranching was doing to the environment. *Really* worried.

Cody closes the notebook, slides it back in with the binders.

"If Wayne knew about this it would piss him off big-time."

~

We're at the island, lying on our stomachs in the sun on a beach towel. We tied the canoe to a bush at the edge of the water, then we swam right around the island, out past the lily pads in the cool, deep water. Cody's a strong swimmer but I am, too.

We floated on our backs, letting the water wash away all the horrible images: the Bible, the blood, the loneliness of the yurt.

After we stretched out in the sun, we exchanged two important facts:

Carlee's just an old friend.

Jason's just a new friend. (I've finally figured that out.)

Then we talked about our families. More about Cody's family than mine, but that's just me.

Stephanie's parents moved away a year after the accident. They couldn't stand living in Aspen Lake anymore. They used to send birthday and Christmas presents, but now it's just an envelope with money and a card.

Jesse's parents are awesome. Cody calls them Gran and Grandad. I told him names are important. Cody and Jesse live in a trailer on their ranch.

Jesse has someone, a nurse in Hundred Mile, Samantha. She's been in their lives since Cody was seven. He thinks of her as his mom, not Stephanie. He hadn't really thought about Stephanie much at all until they did a show last summer about the hit and run on *Crime Watchers*.

I tell Cody that Mom had a relationship for about a year with Jane's father but that he never lived with us and a couple of years later he disappeared. End of child support. I tell him that she worked hard and sometimes had two jobs, one in the day and one at night. Crap jobs, she called them.

That she loved horses and libraries.

That she made beautiful origami butterflies.

Now we're discussing tattoos. Cody likes the Celtic knot idea better than the Yggdrasil. "Why would you want a tattoo that no one can pronounce?" he says.

"It's more mysterious?"

He sits up and presses his fingers into the top of my shoulder and then takes them away. "The sunburn test. You're getting fried."

I sigh.

I sit up, too, and pull on my T-shirt. I hug my knees with my arms. The feeling of Cody's hand on my skin is still there. I want to touch his arm, feel *his* skin, which is brown and tight. I want him to touch me again.

A loon pops up right in front of us and makes its eerie cry.

"That's a loon," he says.

"Really? Tell me something I don't know."

"Okay. You've got a mosquito on your face."

He brushes my cheek with his hand and leaves it there. He

leans forward. He smells like sweat and bug spray and cherry coke. His nose bumps against mine. Then our lips find each other. It lasts a long time. It's amazing.

"Now," he says. "I want to check out your horse."

~

I'm lying on my stomach in my bunk, reading. The bedroom door is shut. I need privacy.

Jane flings the door open.

"I thought Jason was your boyfriend," she says.

I grab my pillow, aim, and fire it at her.

She screams and runs.

~

"What are you *doing*, Margaret?" says Jane.

Margaret's in the middle of the lawn, gazing up at the empty blue sky.

"I'm looking for rain clouds," she says.

CHAPTER FORTY-ONE

I'm walking back from the field carrying a bucket with fly spray, a container of something called *Swat*, and rubber gloves. *Swat* is pink gunk that you rub on parts of the horse where the black flies are really chewing—around their ears, under their bellies. It's messy but it works.

Hooves clatter ahead of me. Amber's trotting up the driveway on Champion.

"Hey Rachel! You wanna ride? My client cancelled, so I've got the morning off."

"Sure!"

"Check with Margaret," she says, jumping off at the hitching post.

Margaret and Jane are in Margaret's bed. The curtains are pulled and they're both asleep, *Nate the Great* books scattered everywhere.

I close the door softly.

"She said it's okay?" says Amber.

"Yup. It's okay."

~

We ride behind the old chicken house and down a bank. It's a different way than we go with Margaret. We splash across a shallow creek beside a wooden footbridge. Magic picks his way over the rocks carefully. There's one tense moment when he steps into a hole where the water's deeper. He stumbles, gets his balance back, and we're on the other side. We cross two fields and then we're in the forest.

It looks like we're following an old road, buried under long grass. We cross a patch of hard, dried mud with a deep rut in it that was probably made by a tire. No one's driven up here for a long time, though, because little bushes are growing in the middle and there are two places where we have to thrash our way around fallen trees.

It's wide enough to ride side by side. We're climbing now. Amber does all the talking, about why she and Cassie's father split up, how hard the real estate course was, her plans to get out of Hundred Mile. I'd be clinically depressed if I had her life, but I can tell she really loves being a mother.

We break out of the trees into bright sunshine. We're in tall grass with patches of blue and red flowers. There's one huge tree at the edge of a steep bank. Below us, a long ribbon of shining water.

"Butterfly Lake," says Amber.

~

"This fir tree is ancient. I bet it's been here for hundreds of years," she says.

Magic and Champion are grazing, their bits jingling, and we're sitting on a carpet of brown needles in the shade of the huge tree. On the opposite side of Butterfly Lake, the forest grows right to the edge and tall trees are reflected upside down in the still water.

It's beautiful.

"This is really a pond, not a lake," says Amber. "But Butterfly Pond doesn't sound as good. Beavers made it." She stands up. "Come on, I'll show you."

The grass is slippery under our boots as we skid down the bank.

Amber points to one end of the pond. "That's actually a beaver dam under all those bushes and grass. It's completely grown over now. But see, it goes right across. A little bit of water gets through and goes all the way to Aspen Lake. That's the creek we rode through by the house."

"Are the beavers still here?" I ask.

"Nope. If there were beavers, you'd see freshly gnawed sticks. There used to be an abandoned beaver lodge here too, right over there on the side, but it's gone now."

She picks up a stone and tosses it into the water. "D'you know something? I haven't been here since…well, since Stephanie died and your mom left. That seems forever ago now. I just never wanted to come back by myself. So, you can feel honored that I've come with you."

"Thank you," I say.

"Your mom told you about Stephanie, I guess."

"Yes." I don't want to tell Amber that Mom never told me anything.

We sit at the bottom of the bank. Bugs with long legs skate across the calm surface of the water.

"It was the best summer ever," she says. "We were all hanging out together. Me and Layla and Steph, Jesse and Jimmy. Layla and Steph were always so tight but they let me be part of it, too. We were eighteen. We'd just graduated. We were so excited about Steph's baby, even though it wasn't exactly planned. Jesse and Steph had started dating in the fall, but it never seemed that serious. And then all of a sudden, they were going to be parents."

"Was Stephanie glad?"

"She was scared at first and she barfed every morning for three months. It was hard at school when she started showing. But I still think she was excited. Then it was summer and everything was perfect. We even built a yurt. It was Jimmy's idea."

She clamps her hand over her mouth. "Shit. I shouldn't even talk about the yurt. That was insensitive."

"That's okay," I say. "I know all about it."

"So, Margaret finally told you?"

"Cody. I've been inside it."

"Oh God. I don't think I could go in there. I *know* I couldn't. Was there anything...?"

Her voice trails off.

Yeah, there's Bible verses on the walls. Blood sprayed all over. All I say is, "I found a CD."

"Oh my God," she says slowly. "You're right. There was a CD. Wayne had a video camera that he never used and Jimmy swiped it one day. We were fooling around with it. I don't remember ever actually watching the video."

She doesn't ask to borrow it.

"I saw Jimmy at the store last summer," she says. "A few weeks before he…well, died. I hadn't seen him for years. He didn't look good. He was ranting on about Armageddon and climate change and methane gas and how we were destroying the planet. It was scary. And sad. He'd changed so much."

She runs a long stalk of grass between her fingers and tiny seeds sprinkle onto her jeans. "We should get going. I've got to show a place this afternoon."

We stand up, brush grass from our legs.

"Look," says Amber, pointing. "Bald eagle."

The eagle is perched on the top of a dead tree. He's huge. His white head gleams in the sun. He surveys his realm. The King of Butterfly Lake.

I can see why Mom loved this place.

We climb up the bank. I don't know what Amber's thinking. If she's sad or happy. She stops suddenly, picks up something in the grass.

"That's weird," she says. "Someone must have been here and dropped this. That is *really* weird."

"Let me see that," I say.

It's a brown leather glove.

There's a jagged rip in the thumb.

Margaret was here.

CHAPTER FORTY-TWO

"You're in BIG TROUBLE," says Jane.

She's at the kitchen table, working on a bead bracelet. There's milk and Chocolate Lucky Charms spilled across the counter.

"Margaret is looking EVERYWHERE for you," she says.

"Where is she now?"

"She's gone back to the lake. I'm supposed to stay right here and not move."

I meet Margaret halfway down the trail to the lake. "Where have you been?" she says. Her voice is quiet, but I know she's furious.

"I went riding with Amber. You were sleeping. I didn't want to disturb you."

"No note, Rachel?"

"I'm sorry. I thought you'd see that Magic was gone."

I'm lying. The horses are turned out in the field by the hayshed this week, out of sight of the house. I didn't leave a note because I prayed I'd be back before she noticed. Because, for some reason, she doesn't want me to go riding with Amber.

But why should I care? Margaret lies to me.

"It's not like I went by myself. I was with Amber."

"Where did you go?"

More lies. "Just some trails. Mostly where we ride with you. I'm sorry. I'm really sorry."

There's sweat on Margaret's forehead. "Nowhere else?" she says.

What would she say if I told her we found her glove at Butterfly Lake? The lake that she said didn't exist.

"No. I *said* I'm sorry."

"Don't ever do that again."

~

Jane and I are on the lawn. It's afternoon but the clouds are so heavy and black, it feels like evening.

"WOO WOO WOO," yells Jane, stamping her feet.

I spin in circles, waving my hands in the air.

Bella throws back her head and howls.

We're doing a rain dance.

~

The first raindrops are splashing into the lake as I paddle to the island.

211

CODY: Wanna come 2 my place on Saturday and play cards?

ME: Sounds good.

CODY: Pick u up at 1:30.

ME: See u.

Two bars, one bar, none. Cody's vanished. It's raining hard now. But I'm grinning as cool water runs into my ears and down my neck.

~

2 A.M.

The rain's pounding on the metal roof. It sounds like it's right above my head. "Can I come up with you?" says Jane in the dark. "Can we read?"

"How come you're still awake?" I switch on the lamp on the wall above me. "Bring *James and the Giant Peach* and your pillow."

We started reading it after dinner and we're already on chapter five. It's one of Mom's books from the box in the old chicken shed. Jane slides under my blanket. Her feet are ice cubes. "Get away from me!" I growl.

"Are you going to read?" says Jane, poking me with a freezing toe.

"I'm warning you!"

"And read extra loud because the rain's so noisy. And please, please, please can I sleep with you tonight?"

Jane's had two dry nights in a row. "Not a chance," I say.

Whenever I read to Jane, she stays perfectly still. She can listen for hours like that. At the end of the chapter, I glance down. She's drifted off her pillow, onto mine. Her eyes are closed. I'll let her stay for a while.

I'm reaching for my book, *The Magician's Nephew.*

"I'm not asleep," she says.

So we start chapter six of *James and the Giant Peach.* That's okay with me. It doesn't matter what the book is. I just need to keep reading.

If I read, I don't have to think about the driver who hit Stephanie and didn't stop. I don't have to think about the blood in the yurt or why Margaret's glove was at Butterfly Lake or why Wayne is so desperate to find that photo. I don't have to think about Mom and why she left.

CHAPTER FORTY-THREE

Margaret's wet riding slicker is hanging in the boot room. She's been out riding early. Fixing fences in the pouring rain? Or did she go back to Butterfly Lake?

I'm not going to ask because she'll only lie.

~

Jesse honks the horn, and I run to his truck so I don't get totally drenched.

Cody jumps out. "Get in fast."

I scramble into the front seat, next to Jesse, and Cody hops back in.

"Hi Rachel. Wet enough for you?" says Jesse.

"It's amazing. It just keeps pouring."

"It's crazy for July. We've had more rain in two days than

we usually get in the whole month of November. We busted the record."

Jesse stops at the store. "I'm going to grab the mail. You guys can pick up some munchies."

Cody gets a giant bag of bright orange cheese curls and a liter bottle of cherry coke.

"You think of anything else?" he says.

I shake my head. "I'm good."

They live in a blue trailer, fifteen minutes from the store, on Jesse's parents' ranch. The trailer is crowded inside but tidy. In the living room, a crocheted afghan hangs on the back of the couch. Firewood is stacked in a wooden box beside a small black woodstove. There's a stack of magazines called *Western Horseman* on the coffee table.

I walk around and look at rodeo photographs on the walls while Cody opens the cheese curls and the cherry coke and hunts for a deck of cards. More photos in frames are arranged on a table—Cody on a horse, Cody and two kids in a boat, Jesse with four smiling women, Cody playing hockey outside.

"We've got lots of family," says Jesse. "I have four sisters. Two live around here and two in town."

I think about the photos in Margaret's room. We were going to look at them together. But we haven't.

Jesse's digging around in a desk drawer in the corner of the room. He pulls out some papers. "I printed this off for you, Rachel," he says. "It's from the Huld Manuscript. It's pretty ancient. Some of it's been translated into English and some of it's in Old Icelandic. There's designs of thirty different magic symbols in here."

He hands me the printed pages. The designs are amazing. They look so old. "Wow, thanks Jesse," I say.

"You're very welcome." He makes coffee and takes it to the couch and picks up a magazine. Cody and I play cards in the kitchen. Fourteen hands of blackjack. Cody polishes off the cheese curls and most of the cherry coke. I eat two apples from a bowl on the counter.

"If it stops raining, I'll show you our horses," says Cody.

It doesn't. The whole time we're playing cards, rain is rattling on the trailer roof. A river pours past the kitchen window. "I'm going outside to unplug the gutter," says Jesse. "Then I'll take a run up to the building supply. You in a hurry to get home, Rachel?"

"No. Any time's good."

He pulls on a black rain slicker. "If I'm not back in an hour, send out a boat," he says, stepping outside into a sheet of rain.

As soon as he leaves, we leap up and wrap our arms around each other. We kiss, long and slow.

When we finally get back to the cards, Cody's supposed to be shuffling, but instead he's flipping a card back and forth.

"You're making me nervous," I say. "What's wrong?"

"That *Crime Watchers* show last summer," he says slowly. "We recorded it. I don't know. I wondered if you wanted to see it."

Cody wants me to say yes.

"Yes," I say.

"Warning," he says. "It's intense."

~

We're on the couch. Cody's fast-forwarding. "There's a bunch of stuff that's not important…. Okay, this is it."

The TV screen fills with a dark highway and rain coming down in slanted sheets. The road is slick and black, glistening with water. It's not quite night, maybe dusk. No lights. Two figures walk along the side of the road.

"That's my dad and my mom," says Cody.

I'm nervous. I tell myself they're *actors*. This is a *re-enactment* to solve a crime. It's a movie. It's not real.

Two people are walking slowly, like they're leaning into the wind. A guy and a girl. The guy drapes something over the girl's shoulders and head. A coat? It's hard to see; it's getting darker and it's raining buckets.

"They went to the mailbox on the corner," says Cody. "They were on their way back. It wasn't like that when they left. Dad said it wasn't even raining. It was a flash Cariboo storm. It came up just like that."

I slip my hand into Cody's.

He leans forward. "This is when the car comes."

It's low, red, speeding toward them.

"A Mazda," he says. "It hydroplanes."

I bite my lip.

There's a huge *thud*. Everything's so black and wet that you can't see what happened. But of course, I know.

"Jesus," says Cody. Every time he watches that, it must be a shock.

Tires squeal. The Mazda swerves, crosses the lane, straightens. Then it's gone.

Headlights appear in the distance, gleaming in the lake of black water that covers the highway, the rain slanting sideways in the lights. A huge semi slows down, brakes grinding. It stops and a man jumps out.

"Get an ambulance," calls a voice.

Cody pushes *stop*.

We sit in silence, my head against his chest. His heart's racing like mine.

"Do you think they'll ever find out who did it?" I say finally.

"I don't know," he says. "It's been so long now. The police found red paint and a piece of broken headlight. They identified it as a Mazda, but no one around here had a car like that."

"After they showed this on TV, did anyone call the police?"

"Yeah, they had some leads but they went nowhere. There was a man in Kamloops who thought he remembered selling a used Mazda to a guy sometime around then. He said there were two people who came, maybe from Aspen Lake. Or Clearwater. He wasn't sure. And he thought it was blue."

"Didn't he keep records?"

"Nah. Around here people sell a lot of stuff under the table. Anyway, he couldn't come up with anything that helped."

"God, Cody. It's so horrible."

"It's really hard for my dad," says Cody. "If they ever find that guy, I don't know what he'll do."

He stands up, pulls me up into his arms.

This time we don't kiss, just hug.

CHAPTER FORTY-FOUR

Someone's knocking at the mudroom door. It's Amber, dripping in a yellow rain slicker, and a woman with frizzy hair, shaking out an umbrella. Amnesty International Kelsey.

I take them into the kitchen where Margaret's making granola bars. It's been a quiet morning. Jane's watching TV with Wayne in the living room, some documentary on tortoises.

"Hello, Mrs. Bird," says Kelsey. "Do you remember me? I'm Kelsey Rainer."

"Yes, I remember you, Kelsey," says Margaret. "I hear you live in Vancouver now. Hello, Amber."

"Hi," says Amber.

Kelsey looks at me. "Hi, Rachel," she says.

"Hey," I say.

"You know each other?" says Margaret.

"Kind of," I say.

"Well." Margaret takes charge. "Is this a social visit or business?"

"Um…," says Amber.

I make a pot of tea because for some reason I'm very nervous. Amber glances around the kitchen. Maybe she's hoping to see signs of packing.

"Now," says Margaret, when we're all sitting down and tea is poured. "What is this all about?"

"I'm up here visiting my family," says Kelsey. "I always come up for the rodeo and stay a couple of weeks. And this time there's something I want…. First, I want to say how sorry I am about Jimmy and Layla."

"Thank you."

"It's hard to know where to start," she says. "I was in contact with Layla for a long time in Vancouver. For years, really. We ran into each other at an Amnesty International meeting way back in 2011. We were so surprised to see each other." Her words pour out. "It was amazing, really. The first time I saw Layla, you were there, too, Rachel. You were really cute. Just a little kid."

Kelsey stops, sips her tea.

"Go on," says Margaret.

"We exchanged phone numbers. I suggested hanging out together, but Layla never wanted to. We'd have coffee once in a while but that was all. Layla wasn't looking for a friend."

"What was she looking for?" asks Margaret.

"Information," says Kelsey. "She asked me to call her every time I came back to Aspen Lake. That's what she was looking for. Someone to tell her about her family."

Nobody says anything.

Amber hops up. "I'll just put the kettle on again," she says.

"Did you know anything about this, Amber?" says Margaret.

"No. I'm hearing this for the first time, too. Kelsey called me last night. She asked me to come with her to see you."

"Mom's on the Friends of Aspen Lake committee with Susan," says Kelsey. "So I'm always up-to-date on what's going on around here. And with your family. Layla…well, she wanted to know everything. All about you and Wayne. But mostly about Jimmy. Did he have a girlfriend? Was he running the ranch with Wayne? Was he still living in the yurt? Stuff like that. And then there was this one time…. A year ago, last spring. I said, Layla, why don't you just go home? And she…."

She stops.

"Yes?" says Margaret.

Kelsey's cheeks flame. "Well, she…. You know, I don't actually think she said anything. I'm not even sure why I brought that up. And then Mom called me a few months later and told me that Jimmy had died. I called Layla. That was the hardest phone call I ever made. I know I was wrong not to tell you where she was, Margaret. I know how much it would have meant to you. I'm so sorry. But she made me promise. I couldn't even tell my mom."

"Well, now you've told me," says Margaret.

"And she did come home, right?" says Kelsey. "She came home when Jimmy died."

"Yes, she did." Margaret stands up. "Now, if you girls—"

"Before we leave," says Amber, "I wanted to have a quick

peek at the bedrooms. I'm wondering if the closets need a fresh coat of paint before we show the house."

"For heaven's sake." Margaret sighs. "Oh, go ahead, Amber. I'll come with you."

I'm waiting for them to leave. Kelsey sips more tea, smiles at me. "It's great to see you, Rachel."

"What were you going to say just then?" I say.

"What?"

"You started to say something about Mom and then you stopped."

"No, I—"

"Yes, you did. When you asked her why she didn't go home. What did my mom say?"

"Oh," says Kelsey. "It really isn't that important. And to be honest, it's probably not something I should even tell you."

"Why?"

Kelsey puts her hands up. "Okay. Layla and I had these conversations. About how great the ranch was and how much she missed everything and how she wished she could see Magic again. This one time she sounded so sad and I finally said, Layla, why don't you just go home? And she said, I can't."

"And then what?"

"She said something terrible had happened one night and it was her fault. She said she wanted a chance to do that night over and that wasn't going to happen, it couldn't. And she couldn't live in a place where that's all she could think about."

"Did she tell you what it was?"

"No. I think she regretted even saying that much. She stopped coming to meetings after that."

Amber's voice comes down the stairs, and then Margaret's. Kelsey jumps up.

She won't meet my eyes. She never mentioned the hit and run. She never said Stephanie's name.

But she knows.

Because it's obvious. It's just *so* obvious.

CHAPTER FORTY-FIVE

Mom killed Stephanie.

I think Wayne got rid of the car. I think Margaret knew. I think Uncle Jimmy knew.

I don't know what to do.

When I've been riding Magic, I've been thinking a lot about Mom. Trying to remember all the good moments. But I won't anymore.

She's ruined everything.

~

CODY: Where are u?
CODY: Why aren't you answering my texts?
CODY: Rachel?

~

Jane's sitting on the edge of her bunk.

"What's up?" I say.

"I don't think I want to go anymore."

"Yes, you do."

Jane's going to Cassie's for her first ever sleepover. It's also the first night we've ever been apart because I don't do sleepovers.

Margaret helped her pack. I check that she's got everything and zip the backpack shut.

"What if I...?" She frowns. "You know."

"You've gone four nights in a row. That's a record. And if something happens, it's not the end of the world. And Susan's really nice. She won't get mad."

"Can I take Hoodie?"

"He's in there. Come on, kiddo. Margaret wants to say good-bye."

Margaret's lying down in the dark. Another migraine. She's blaming it on the atmospheric pressure. The barometer's right at the bottom.

"Are you ready to go?" she says.

"I guess so," says Jane.

"Good. Now, you have a wonderful time and tell me all about it when you get back."

"I love you, Margaret," says Jane.

"I love you, too," says Margaret.

~

Susan's wearing a red rain cape that floats around her like a tent. Cassie's with her, in a pink raincoat and pink gum boots, hopping up and down. Jane's forgotten she doesn't want to go. The two of them are talking a mile a minute.

Susan talked to Margaret on the phone last night. She knows about her migraine. She's brought a frozen lasagna for our dinner and a plastic bag with a package from Amazon and Margaret's mail, two letters, and a seed catalogue with tulips and daffodils on the front.

"You girls go and get in the truck," she says to Cassie and Jane. "Scoot fast so you don't get soaked. I'm just going to pop in on Margaret."

I make Jane put on her ladybug rain jacket, which is hanging in the mudroom. She flies outside after Cassie. When Susan comes back downstairs, I say, "Margaret doesn't want to eat anything."

"She won't until the worst is over. She's a veteran of migraines. She'll be alright. Just check in once in a while. And, Rachel, she said to tell you to open the package. It's for you. She asked me to order it."

I put the lasagna in the oven. Then I pull the little cardboard tab on the package. There's a book inside. *Easy Origami.*

~

This is how you make an origami dog:

Fold in half.
Rotate.
Fold ears down.
Fold behind.
Dog.

To be exact, a dog's head with two floppy ears. It doesn't have a body. I show it to Bella. She yawns and crawls under the kitchen table, flopping onto my feet. I skim through the book for something else with six or less steps.

Fold in half.
Valley fold.
Fold up.
Turn over.
Fold behind.
Rabbit.

Concentrate on the origami.
Don't think about anything else.
I've made a small zoo. A red dog, a yellow rabbit, a pink fox, a purple pelican, a green pig, an orange cat. I'm up to ten steps.

I dig a fork into the lasagna. Still cold in the middle. I find a felt pen in a jar on the counter and draw eyes on the origami animals. Then I go back to the book, flip pages and stop at the frog. Something jars in my brain. A memory of Mom and Jane and me, waiting for ages for our food in a restaurant. Jane, standing up in her chair, then tipping over and crashing onto the floor. Jane howling, making everyone in the restaurant turn and look.

Then what happened?

Mom made a frog out of the paper placemat. She made the frog jump over the napkin holder.

Jane laughed in the middle of her tears. "Do it again."

That's it. I don't remember anything before or after. But the frog is so vivid, it's like it happened yesterday.

The frog in this book has fourteen steps. I pick up a piece of yellow paper with green polka dots. There are lots of *folds, unfolds, turns, pull out the corners, turn over.*

At the end, it says *Push down on the back and the frog will jump.*

My frog jumps over the fox and the pig and onto Bella, who's crawled out from under the table to socialize. I gather up all the animals, take them upstairs, and put them on Jane's bunk.

You made a frog jump over a napkin holder, Mom, and we all laughed, and all that time, you knew what you had done.

Margaret's still sleeping. I dish out the lasagna and tap on Wayne's door.

~

4 A.M.

It's dead quiet. The rain has finally stopped. I turn on my light and swing down onto the floor. Seven pairs of eyes are watching me from Jane's bunk. I arrange the animals in a circle with the frog in the middle. Then I head downstairs and out to the verandah.

It's bright outside with a huge full moon. It doesn't feel like the middle of the night. I can see right across the field below the house. I could walk all the way to the lake without a flashlight.

The moonlight is shining on the Butterfly House. I go inside. Stephanie's butterfly is silver, and the wings are like an angel's. Maybe that's what Mom wanted. An angel for Stephanie.

I squeeze my eyes shut, pushing away this sudden feeling of drowning that washes through me. It keeps happening, ever since I figured out the truth.

I close the glass door behind me and step down onto the grass. It's soaked from the rain, cold on my bare toes.

Then the noise hits me. A roar, thunder, coming from the little creek behind the old chicken shed. I run across the wet grass and stand above the creek. What used to be the creek. The creek that I rode across on Magic is now a raging river.

A torrent of water heaves between the banks. The foot bridge has washed away and only the end supports stick out of the water. A huge log smashes against a boulder, twirls, and is swept downstream. An entire tree, its bark gleaming white in the moonlight, hurtles by. More stuff follows, chunks of wood and thick branches with green leaves.

Amber said that this is the creek that comes from Butterfly Lake. I watch for a while and, shivering, go back to the house.

CHAPTER FORTY-SIX

I don't wake up until nine. Sun is streaming through the window. I go straight outside to the creek.

Except for a bird chirping loudly in the middle of a bush, it's deadly quiet. I could wade across it easily this morning. It would barely be up to my knees.

But I didn't imagine last night. It's a war zone. There's a mess of twigs, branches stripped of their leaves, and small logs tossed up on the grass. There are huge gouges in the banks and a black, muddy line where the water washed over the grass. Small bushes are smashed down. Even the supports for the foot bridge poking out of the water last night are gone.

I go back inside. I eat a bowl of Rice Krispies and then I make scrambled eggs and take a tray to Wayne.

"We need to look for the photo again," he says.

"I'll help you," I say. "Today. I promise."

I make tea and toast an English muffin for Margaret who's sitting up in bed, her curtains pulled shut. The worst of her migraine is over, and she says she'll eat the English muffin. "Is it a nice morning?" she asks. "I think the rain stopped around midnight."

"It's really nice. It's sunny."

"I'll try to get up in the afternoon. I'll stay here for now."

I take my book to the verandah but I can't focus.

I'm going to Butterfly Lake. I'm not leaving a note. I'm just going.

~

When I get Magic from the field, I tell myself, He's just a horse. He doesn't matter anymore.

But that's not true. When I'm brushing him and his eyes go sleepy, I love him.

His feet make a loud clomping sound on the driveway. I glance nervously at Margaret's window as we pass the house, but the curtains stay shut. I ride across the grass, behind the chicken shed, and down the bank to the creek. There's still tons of debris and Magic has to pick his way across. We splash through the water.

My first solo ride. I don't want to screw up. I cross the two fields, trying to relax in the saddle and at the same time, stay alert. Margaret says that when both the rider and the horse are daydreaming, that's when trouble happens.

Magic stops, stiffens his neck and pricks his ears forward. What does he see that I don't? My hands tighten on the reins, and I brace myself. I make myself take a few deep breaths, then slowly loosen my grip, and urge Magic forward gently with my legs. He lowers his head and steps out again.

I can do this. I *am* doing this. I'm riding Magic by myself.

When we get to the edge of the forest, it takes me a few minutes to find the old road hidden under the long grass. Magic stumbles in one of the ruts, and I tumble forward onto his neck. I sit up, adjust the reins, and we start to climb.

We come out of the trees, shade into sun, through the long grass to the ancient tree. There's a strange smell and I don't know what I'm expecting to see but that fear washes over me again.

Butterfly Lake is gone.

My breath catches in my throat.

There's a sea of mud. In the middle, splattered with black gunk and weeds, sunken to the tops of its tires, is a car.

My heart is hammering so hard that it aches. I jump to the ground, hook Magic's reins to the saddle, and let him loose. I slide down the grassy bank to the edge of the mud. I'm not good at judging distances but I'd guess the car is about three meters from me. It's tilted on one side and the door on the front passenger side is hanging open. There are enough bare spots in the mud where I can see the color.

Red.

I swallow sour bile in the back of my throat.

There's a shrill screech. The bald eagle is still here. He swoops down into the grass, then soars up into the sky, a limp body dangling from his beak.

He's back in his tower now, watching over his kingdom. Guarding the car. Protecting our family.

The King of Butterfly Lake.

But Butterfly Lake has washed away.

Tears pour down my cheeks. I can't stay here any longer. I should never have come. I climb back up the slope and catch Magic. I fumble with the reins and my leg buckles when I swing up into the saddle. I don't look back.

～

I'm lying on my bunk, staring at the ceiling.

"I called Susan to check on Jane," says Margaret. She's standing in our bedroom door in her dressing gown and slippers. She hasn't been outside. She doesn't know anything. The dark circles under her eyes look like shadows.

"Jane's having a wonderful time," she says. "Their springer spaniel Molly has a new litter of puppies, and Susan says that Jane is enchanted."

"That's nice."

"She's going to stay over one more night."

"Right."

I pick up my book.

"Did you and Wayne have any lunch?"

"No. I wasn't hungry."

Margaret waits. Maybe she wants me to apologize for not getting Wayne something to eat. I want her to go away. I want to be by myself.

She shuts the door and leaves.

I'm part of it now. I'm part of this family's secret.

CHAPTER FORTY-SEVEN

I ride again in the afternoon. To be with Magic. To get out of the house.

This time, I tell Margaret I'm going, and she hesitates, and I think she's going to say no. But in the end, she just says, "Be careful."

Magic and I wander. I know my way around the ranch now. We go down to the old homestead and the marsh, back along the Woodpecker Trail, through some hayfields and then to the hill where Margaret and Jane and I had the picnic. I slide off Magic's back and let him eat grass.

I sit for a long time looking down at the ranch and the lake. Thinking.

When I get back, Margaret's in her garden, watering.

"I've been to Butterfly Lake," I say. "It's gone. It's just mud now. The beaver dam broke."

Margaret's face turns white. She puts her watering can on the ground. "I looked at the creek," she says slowly. "All the debris everywhere. I knew it had to be the dam."

"I saw the car."

"Rachel, we need to talk."

"No."

"Yes, we do. Please, Rachel."

Silently we walk back to the house and sit on the verandah near the Butterfly House.

"Jimmy saw an ad for a used car in Kamloops," says Margaret.

She must have told this story to herself a thousand times. Gone over and over it. That's what I would've done. Like I do with the day Jane burned herself and we ended up in a foster home. But this is so much worse. Stephanie was killed.

"A red Mazda. He asked your mom to go with him to drive it back. He wasn't allowed to drive because his license had been suspended for drinking and driving. They hitchhiked to Kamloops and were home by the late afternoon. We didn't know they'd gone. I was at a quilting retreat, and Wayne was helping Martin with a colicky horse."

I stare at the butterflies. All the colors blur and swirl and I blink hard.

"Jimmy wanted to drive the car around Aspen Lake, show it to one of his friends. Your mom was in her room with her headphones on, listening to music. She had no idea Jimmy wanted to take the car out again. She said she didn't even hear him leave."

Something huge shifts inside me.

"What did you just say?"

"Your mom said she didn't hear Jimmy leave," she says.

"He went by himself?"

"Yes."

"Mom didn't drive?"

"No."

"You're sure?"

"Yes, Jimmy drove himself."

"But I thought—" My throat closes.

"That your mom hit Stephanie? Rachel. Listen to me. She didn't go with Jimmy. She was home, listening to music. She didn't go."

I burst into tears.

"Oh, Rachel," says Margaret. "Come here."

I shake my head no. I press the heels of my hands into my eyes, waiting until my tears stop. I should feel so relieved, but I don't. I'm just so tired. Of everything.

"Should I keep talking?" says Margaret.

"Yes. But don't lie. Please don't lie."

Margaret looks stricken. "This is the truth. Jimmy's friend wasn't home, so he turned around. There was a storm. It was so sudden. It was getting dark and it was raining so hard he couldn't see a thing. He hit Stephanie, right by the mailboxes. He said he thought he'd hit a deer."

"But he didn't stop," I say.

"No."

"Why?"

Margaret shakes her head. "In the morning, Martin called and said that Stephanie had been hit the night before on the highway and was in the hospital. That she was badly hurt. She was with Jesse. They were by the mailboxes. Wayne knew right away it was Jimmy. He'd seen the car and he'd seen the broken headlight."

"Were you there?"

"No. I heard about Stephanie later that day, at the quilting retreat. I came right home. Wayne was out by the hay shed, washing the tractor. I remember thinking that was odd. Jimmy was in the yurt, and your mom was in her room. She was in a terrible state. She told me that Wayne had asked Jimmy if anyone knew he had the car. Jimmy said no, no one had seen him. And then he told your mom and Jimmy to stay inside the house. Not to answer the phone. They heard the tractor. He was gone for hours. When he came back, he said he had taken care of the car. He said they would never talk about it again."

"Why?" I say. "Why would he do that?"

"Because he believed that if he didn't, it would destroy the Bird family."

"What are you going to do?"

"I'm going to call Rob. And then I'm going to call the police."

～

3 A.M.

"I found the car eight years ago," says Margaret. "It was a summer just like this. So hot and dry. I used to love riding to Butterfly Lake to think about your mom. For some peace. I never imagined the car was in there."

"Where did you think it was?"

"I didn't let myself think. And then, that summer, the water level dropped and I saw it. It was a terrible shock."

"It was for me, too," I say.

"I know."

"You've been praying for rain," I say, "so no one would find the car, but it rained too much."

"Maybe not," says Margaret. "Maybe it's time. That first week after the accident, I told myself over and over that Stephanie was going to be okay. When she died, I was overwhelmed. With emotion, with grief, with fear. That's not an excuse. I'm not trying to find excuses."

"I'll never understand why Wayne did it. And why you agreed to it."

"I can't tell you exactly what Wayne was thinking at the time. For me, it was about our children. I'd already lost Rob. He left as soon as he graduated. He went as far away as he could. He had no real interest in the ranch and Wayne couldn't accept that. I'd lost your mom. She said she hated us. Wayne, for hiding the car, Jimmy for killing Stephanie, me for not fixing everything. That's what mothers are supposed to do. Fix things. But I didn't know how to fix this."

Bella pads across the room and rests her head on Margaret's lap.

"I couldn't lose Jimmy, too," says Margaret. "Of all my children, Wayne was hardest on Jimmy. He would have gone to jail—he had a previous conviction for drinking and driving. I couldn't bear that. He needed me the most to protect him."

Bella flops on her back and Margaret rubs her tummy gently with her foot. "I knew in a few days that we had made a terrible mistake. But your mother had gone and it seemed too late. And it would have destroyed Wayne and I couldn't do that."

"Did you ever think of telling someone?" I ask.

Margaret nods. "So many times I drove to Hundred Mile, planning to go to the police station. I'd get as far as the parking lot and turn around. I think Susan and Martin suspect. Jimmy wasn't drinking when he hit Stephanie. It's the only thing that gives me a little bit of comfort. Since his conviction, he had never touched alcohol. I couldn't bear it if he had killed Stephanie because he was drunk."

I almost tell Margaret that I know what really happened to Uncle Jimmy. That it wasn't an accident. That he shot himself deliberately in the yurt. But it all seems too hard to say right now. And I don't tell her my other thought. That maybe telling the truth would have saved Uncle Jimmy's life.

"Cody is Stephanie's son," I say.

"Yes," says Margaret.

"He's going to hate me forever."

"Oh Rachel. You don't know that."

"Yes, I do."

~

4 A.M.

I'm lying on my bunk, staring at the ceiling. Again.

Why did Mom tell Kelsey that something terrible had happened and it was her fault?

Why did she say she wanted a chance to do that night over?

CHAPTER FORTY-EIGHT

I carry a tray with two fried eggs and a strip of bacon to Wayne's room. He's slumped in his armchair. He doesn't look good. Margaret has told him about the car.

I set the tray on his desk. There's a piece of paper in the old typewriter and a few more papers in a pile beside it.

I pick them up. "What's this?"

"What do you think it is? Chapter One."

"You're really going to write this thing? Still? How can you even think about it?"

He grunts.

I take the yurt key out of my pocket and hold it up. "I've locked the yurt. I'm returning the key."

I can feel him watching my back as I open the top right desk drawer and drop the key inside.

"Jimmy was going to destroy this ranch," he says. "He

was full of crap about the environment. If raising cattle isn't sustainable, you tell me how come our family has been doing it for three generations? And making a hell of a success of it! And then Jimmy had the gall to accuse me of not managing my land properly. *My* land."

"You mean the Birds' land. Not just yours."

"Listen to me," says Wayne. "You suddenly care so much about this ranch? Jake Simons phoned me last summer. We've ranched together in Aspen Lake for fifty years. He said, was it true? Was Jimmy selling the cows, looking into sheep or poultry?"

"It doesn't matter now," I say. "Your cows are gone."

"I was finished with Jimmy. I went to the yurt. I told him he had one week to clear off. Get out of Aspen Lake. I hid that damn car to save him and then all these years later, he stabbed me in the back. Sheep on the Bird ranch? Over my dead body."

"You hid the car because you couldn't stand the thought of anyone thinking the Birds weren't perfect." My entire body is trembling.

"Get out," says Wayne. "Leave me alone!"

I pause at the door. "You took all this away from Uncle Jimmy, everything that mattered to him, and then you just left him alone in the yurt? Did you know he had all those guns?"

"Of course he had guns. This is a ranch. He had hunting rifles."

"So what happened? Did you hear a shot?"

Wayne leans over, buries his head in his hands. His shoulders heave up and down.

"No." I can barely hear him. "But Margaret did."

~

Out the kitchen window, an RCMP van towing a trailer loaded with two ATVs is parked in front of the tack room. Two men in uniforms are getting out, looking around.

I call Bella and leave through the verandah door.

It's sunny today, but not hot like it was, and there's a little breeze. I sit on the bank with my feet in the water. I stare at the canoe and think about when Cody and I went to the island.

It was my last perfect day.

If the dam hadn't broken, the car would still be hidden. There'd be no police officers on our ranch.

I find a stick and throw it in the water for Bella to fetch. She swims out and grabs it, circles, and swims back. She drops it at my feet, her tail wagging. Then she shakes and drenches my legs.

I throw the stick over and over again.

Bella will do that forever, Margaret said. Maybe Bella and I can just stay here forever and never go back to the house.

After a few more throws, I tell Bella to jump in the canoe with me and I paddle right around the island. I focus on my strokes, long hard ones, one after the other, pushing away everything else. My arms ache and I let the canoe drift, trailing my fingers in the cool water.

In the distance is the yurt. Did Uncle Jimmy kill himself because of Stephanie? Did he kill himself because Wayne told him he had to leave the ranch? Maybe he felt like I do sometimes, that everything is too hard, and, for him the feeling just got so terrible he couldn't bear it.

Bella decides she's had enough and starts barking. I paddle back. She leaps out a couple of meters from the shore and the canoe wobbles and almost capsizes. As I pull the canoe up onto the bank, she shakes hard, spraying water all over me. We head back to the house.

The RCMP van is still here. There's a ramp at the back of the trailer and the ATVs are gone.

Uncle Rob's blue BMW is parked behind the van.

~

There's a map on the kitchen table, empty mugs. Uncle Rob's making coffee. He crushes me in a bear hug. He hasn't shaved and his face is rough, but I hug him back. It's the first time I've ever given Uncle Rob a proper hug. I start to cry.

"Hey, Rach."

We lean into each other. I'm soaking his shirt, but I know he won't care. I wipe my eyes.

"Coffee?" he says.

"I don't drink coffee."

"Right. I forgot. Caffeine's bad for you."

We both laugh. My nose is running, and I pick up a napkin. "Where's Margaret?"

"She's with Dad. This whole thing has been a horrible shock, and Dad just doesn't do well with shock."

Uncle Rob carries his mug and a handful of Margaret's raisin cookies to the table. "My breakfast," he says.

He sounds so ordinary. So…Uncle Rob. I sit across from him. "Did you talk to the police?"

"Yes. I got here just before they went out to look at the car. I showed them where to go on the map."

"What's going to happen?"

"They'll have to get the car towed out of there. They asked about a tractor and I told them I'd get Martin to bring his over. I also talked to a friend of mine in Vancouver. He's a criminal lawyer and he's very good. The best. I want to make sure we do everything right. Margaret's going to talk to Susan and Martin."

"What about Jesse?" I say. I'm terrified.

"Not yet," he says. "I can't tell Jesse something like this on the phone. I'm going to go over to his place as soon as I can. Today."

Cody will know today.

"Rob!" yells Margaret from the doorway. "There's something wrong with your father."

CHAPTER FORTY-NINE

Uncle Rob phones for an ambulance.

He's pacing between Wayne's bedroom and the kitchen window. "It's going to take forever," he says. "We've got to get Dad in the car. We can meet the ambulance halfway."

Wayne can just barely walk with Margaret supporting him on one side and Uncle Rob on the other. His face is gray and wet with sweat, he staggers a lot and keeps stopping. He gasps for air.

Uncle Rob and Margaret slide him into the back seat of the car. I've grabbed a blanket and a bottle of water. Uncle Rob tucks the blanket over Wayne. "Breathe," I say. "Five in, five out. Come on, Wayne. Please."

His eyes are closed, and he's slumped over, and oh my God I don't think he even hears me. "Call Susan, Rachel," says Margaret. "Her number's in that little book by the phone. Tell her that I'll call her from Hundred Mile. Ask her to keep Jane with them."

The car disappears down the driveway. Everything is falling apart around me. I'm shaking so hard. Jane and I have just found our family. We lost Mom but we can't lose anyone else. We just can't. Not Uncle Rob. Not Margaret. Not Wayne.

I couldn't bear it. Not now.

~

Wayne had a heart attack.

Uncle Rob and Margaret get back at five o'clock. I've fed Bella and I'm making spaghetti for dinner. I don't know if we'll even eat it, but it was something to do. Margaret's been on the phone with Susan for a long time. When she comes for dinner, her face is gray.

We pick at the spaghetti as Uncle Rob gives me information. It's a minor heart attack. Wayne might have to go to a bigger hospital in Kamloops. It's not certain when he'll be home.

No one wants dessert but Margaret thaws a frozen lemon cake in the microwave.

It's something to do.

She's just put some slices on a plate when we hear the mudroom door crash open. Jane runs into the kitchen with an apologetic-looking Susan behind her.

"She said she wants Rachel," says Susan.

Jane catapults into my lap and I hang on to the edge of the table so we don't topple over. She grabs a slice of lemon cake.

"Hey, Uncle Rob!" she says.

"Hey, Jane!"

"What are you doing back here?" I say. "I thought you were staying another night."

"Can I have one of Molly's puppies, Margaret?" she says. "Please, please, please?"

~

Uncle Rob says he's going out for a while. He doesn't say where, but I know he's going to Jesse and Cody's trailer.

CHAPTER FIFTY

Jane and I are in the kitchen and I've got the origami paper and the book. I'm going to show her how to make a dog. While she's choosing her paper, I say, "Something happened while you were gone. Wayne had a heart attack and he's in the hospital."

"Oh," says Jane.

She's careful folding and when she's done, she starts drawing a nose and eyes on her dog with the felt pen.

After a long time, she says, "Like when Mom went to the hospital when she took that drug?"

"Well, not like that. He's going to be okay."

"But it's scary."

"Yeah, it is."

"How long will he be there?"

"I don't know."

Jane puts her felt pen down. "Why did he have a heart attack?"

"It just happened."

~

7 P.M.

Jane can't stop crying. She's in the top bunk with me, wrapped in my arms.

"I don't want Wayne to die," she says.

"He won't."

The scar on the tip of her nose is white.

"I want Mom," she sobs.

I hold her tight.

"Me too."

~

Uncle Rob finds me in the pasture with the horses. He gives me one of his new Uncle Rob hugs.

My heart's pounding. "What did Jesse say?"

"Not too much, really. He was so shocked. He's going to need time for this to sink in, for sure. He just kept saying, 'Jimmy? I can't believe it.'"

"What did Cody say?"

"He didn't say anything."

250

~

Just before bed, Uncle Rob and I take Bella for a walk along the road. She's been searching for Wayne all day and whining at the door to his room.

Jane's fast asleep in my bunk. Susan's drinking tea with Margaret on the verandah. Uncle Rob's been talking to the doctor in Hundred Mile.

Now it's just me and him.

The sky is filling with stars.

"Do you really believe Wayne is going to be alright?" I ask.

"Yes. They might have to move him to Kamloops but he's going to survive this. He's tough." He sounds so sure, and it helps. But there's all the other stuff too.

"Can't you make your friend come any sooner? The lawyer?"

"John Higgs. He's tied up with a trial. I've tried but Sunday's the best he can do."

"What will happen first?"

"Dad will have to make a formal statement to the police. He's going to have to answer a lot of hard questions. They'll want to talk to Margaret. And to me, too. I've known for almost a year what happened, and I chose not to do anything. And, of course, they'll notify Stephanie's parents."

"Will the police go to the hospital to talk to Wayne?"

"Yes. But John will be with him. Then the prosecutor will decide if they're going to press charges."

It sounds terrifying. "Could Wayne go to prison?"

"God, I hope not. It was such a long time ago. We can pray that will make a difference."

"I can't imagine this ranch without Wayne," I say.

"Me neither." Uncle Rob picks up a stick and tosses it for Bella.

"I'm going to have the yurt taken down. I meant to do it right after Jimmy died but…I don't know. So much just got in the way."

"You should have told me," I say. "About Uncle Jimmy, about Stephanie. It would've been so much easier if I'd known."

"You're right. I'm sorry. I wasn't sure what to do. You and Jane have been through so much."

"I still wish you'd told me."

He takes my hand.

"Aleksandra's gone back to Poland," he says.

"Really?"

"She was offered a position in a very good hospital, working with cancer patients. It's what she's good at."

"Are you going too?"

"Not right now."

He tilts his head back. "Look at all those stars."

"They're beautiful."

"I grew up here and I can't name even one constellation. I wish I'd paid more attention."

"To the stars?"

"To everything."

~

5 A.M.

"What happened when Mom came here when Uncle Jimmy died?" I ask.

Margaret's sewing little glass buttons on Jane's sweater. She sets it down in her lap.

"Well, she phoned from the bus depot in Hundred Mile."

"Was Uncle Rob already here?"

"Yes. He'd gotten in from Poland the day before and rented a car at the airport and drove straight up here."

"And he didn't know anything?"

"No. I used to send him letters with bits of news. He knew Wayne and Jimmy had been running the ranch. He knew your mom had you and Jane. I'd never told him the truth. But I told him everything that night."

"What did he say?"

"He was furious at first. I've never seen him so angry. And he was very upset about your mom. He said he'd been trying to find her on social media."

"Mom hated things like Facebook."

"She came up on a night bus," says Margaret. "She called us from the bus depot in the morning. Uncle Rob was exhausted, but he got right back in the car and rushed off to town to pick her up."

"What was Mom like when she was here?"

"Restless. She smoked cigarette after cigarette. That was new. She never smoked when she was a teenager. The first day, she got up early in the morning and went for a long ride on Magic. It calmed her down a little."

Mom and Magic.

"She phoned you really early, on the second day, and she must have talked to you because she said everything was fine. She didn't tell me she'd left you alone in the apartment. She called again in the afternoon and there was no answer and then she kept calling every ten minutes. She tried Crystal, too. She was frantic. Finally, Rob drove her back to Hundred Mile to catch the night bus to Vancouver. We didn't even know what had happened."

"How did you find out?"

"She called Rob from the hospital. She said Jane had been burned, and they were keeping her at the hospital for a few days. But that everything was under control."

Under control? We went straight to the foster home.

"I prayed she'd at least stay in touch with Rob," says Margaret. "But her call from the hospital was the last time he spoke to her."

She picks up the sweater, fiddles with a button.

"I only had your mom for two days, but I had that." She adds softly, "I knew she wasn't going to come back."

CHAPTER FIFTY-ONE

Four RCMP officers come in the morning, this time with four ATVs on the trailer. A green truck with *Aspen Lake Towing* on the side follows them. The back is flat and open. It's for the car. I'm glad Jane's not watching this. She's in Margaret's bed, reading *Nate the Great* books.

Martin's driving a huge tractor, which he parks behind the tow truck. He jumps down to talk to Uncle Rob and the tow truck driver, a man with a red cap that says *Bill* on it. When everything is organized and the RCMP officers, Bill, and Martin have left for Butterfly Lake, Uncle Rob gets a phone call from the hospital.

"It looks like Wayne's staying in Hundred Mile," he says. "That's good news. I'll take you in, Mom, to see him."

At the last minute, Margaret fusses about leaving us.

"We'll be fine," I say. "Go."

~

They drive away.

The phone rings and rings and rings.

I've become Margaret.

I'm too scared to answer it.

~

I pack a picnic and take Jane to the island. She hardly says a word the whole way there. I spread our towels on the flat rock, and we plunk down. We pull off our T-shirts. Jane's wearing her red polka dot bathing suit and I'm in my purple tanning bikini.

She looks so skinny. I take the sunscreen out of the backpack, flip the cap, and pour a big dollop onto Jane's left shoulder. I smooth it down her arm. Then I move to her right shoulder. My fingers falter on the burned skin, then I rub in the cream.

When I'm finished, I say, "Can you put some on my back?"

"I guess so."

I put the sunscreen down. "Come here, kiddo."

She snuggles into me. "Everything's really weird around here right now, isn't it?" I say.

"I don't get why there's a police car at our house," she says. "And that tow truck."

"They're going to get something."

"What?"

"An old car."

"Where is it?" she says. "On our ranch?"

"Yeah."

"What do they want it for?"

"They want to look at it."

"Why?"

"They're trying to see if it's the same car that they've been trying to find."

She sighs. "Okay."

She digs through the backpack. "Apples, bananas," she recites in a very gloomy voice. "Granola bars—hey! Viva Puffs!"

I reach for one. The chocolate coating is sticky. And how do they make it so perfectly smooth and round?

"There's a marshmallow inside that," says Jane. "And red jam."

~

CODY: Where are u?

~

I see it first. The red car, sitting on the back of the tow truck. It's held there by chains. Jane's too busy talking about the new puppies at Susan and Martin's house to notice. Then she stops mid-breath. "Is that the car?"

It's too late to take her the other way.

"Yeah," I say.

"What's that yucky smell?"

"Mud."

It's everywhere. On the car, on the chains, on the ATVs.

The tractor is parked to one side, splattered with mud. More mud is caked on its enormous black tires.

Martin's talking to an RCMP officer. Another officer is stripping off green rubber boots that are attached to rubber pants that go right up to his chest. They're coated in mud.

Slimy green weeds drape the roof of the car and dangle from the bumpers. A piece of yellow rope ties the passenger door shut. The tires are so flat you can barely see them.

Bill walks around the car, adjusting chains. Martin shakes hands with the RCMP officer and walks over to Jane and me.

"What will happen to it?" I say.

"It's part of a criminal investigation now."

"What does that mean?" says Jane.

Martin looks uncomfortable. But I always tell Jane everything she wants to know. "It's okay," I say. "You can talk about it."

"First they've got to make sure it's the right car," he says. "The police collected evidence at the scene. Broken glass from the headlight, paint chips, bits of metal. They'll take the car to Kamloops and run it through a bunch of tests. It's called forensics."

"Like on TV," says Jane.

"That's right," says Martin. "They'll look at where Stephanie was walking along the highway and the direction the car was traveling and make sure the damage on the car matches the impact."

"What's impact mean?" says Jane.

He looks at me. "Where the car hit Stephanie."

"Who's Stephanie?" says Jane.

"Remember?" I say. "She was Mom's best friend."

"And the car hit her?"

"Yes."

"Is she dead?" she says.

"Yes."

Bill starts the tow truck. The ATVs are loaded, and the RCMP officers are in their van. The officer in the passenger seat unrolls the window and calls to Martin. "Thanks again for all your help. Tell the Birds we'll be in touch."

Martin raises his hand, and we watch them leave. Even with all the mud, I can see the smashed headlight and the dented fender.

The red car has no more secrets.

~

2 A.M.

We're awake. Me, Jane, Margaret.

We're the night wanderers.

CHAPTER FIFTY-TWO

Wayne's asked for some of his papers, so he has something to look at in the hospital. A nurse told Uncle Rob that he's the worst patient she's ever had. Margaret said he must be feeling better.

I gather up Chapter One. If you can even call it that. The typewriter seems to be missing *b*, *s*, *r*, *k*, and *t*, and there's white stuff smeared everywhere on the pages. I look around and spot a three-hole punch and a stack of binders on one of the bookshelves. I punch the papers and sort through the binders to see if there's an empty one.

They're labelled *cattle sales, feed store orders, warranties, parts for the John Deere tractor, grazing licenses.*

Loose papers spill all over the floor. I bend down to pick them up. Under a pile of receipts from Hundred Mile Feed is a photograph.

It's Uncle Jimmy, standing in front of a red car.

He's holding a beer bottle.

I've found it, the last photo in Mom's camera. I look at the beer bottle, and my heart starts to thud.

Why did Wayne keep the photo? To remind Uncle Jimmy? To remind himself? No. They would never forget. I don't know why he kept it. But I do understand why Margaret cannot see this. She believes that Jimmy wasn't drinking when he killed Stephanie. She's holding onto that for dear life.

I tear the photo into pieces, go into the kitchen, open a lid on top of the woodstove, and drop them into the flames.

~

ME: Can you come over? I need to talk to you.

CODY: Picking up hay bales for my grandfather. I'll come right after.

~

In the afternoon, Margaret, Uncle Rob, Jane, and I go to the Aspen Lake cemetery. It's on a hill, looking over the lake, surrounded by a white picket fence. It's pretty here, with big leafy trees, ferns, and vines, and grass sprinkled with white daisies.

We start in the older part where there are lots of crumbled stone crosses and old worn gravestones. We walk slowly and Margaret tells us what she knows. She shows us where Daryl and Daphne Bird are buried. Their names and dates are worn into the mossy gray stone and we can just make them out. Daryl was born in 1887, Daphne in 1898. They died together, August 10, 1966.

"A fire," says Margaret. "At Daryl's brother's house in Clinton. They were stopping over for a night. Wayne was thirteen. He remembers when they got the news."

There's something written at the bottom of the gravestone, but the words have no edges. They've eroded into the old stone. Lost forever.

Nearby, Wayne's parents, Joseph and Mary Bird, share one gravestone. *Say not in grief they are no more, but live in thankfulness that they were.* Jane stumbles over *grief* but she can read that.

"After Joseph died, your great-grandmother Mary lived with us," says Margaret. "She and your mom were very close. Mary would have helped us. She'd seen everything in her life, and she was very wise."

Uncle Rob is standing, hands in his pockets, gazing at the lake. He said he needs some time alone. Margaret, Jane, and I keep wandering.

Margaret likes talking about the Birds.

We find a Bird who didn't come back from World War I. *Matthew Bird 1898–1917. Lest We Forget.* He was nineteen. One of Daryl's younger brothers.

Elizabeth Sarah Bird 1880–1940. Dearly beloved wife of Randolph James Bird. Randolph, Daryl's cousin.

There are Bird children too, buried in this cemetery. *Daniel Bird, 1901–1907. Our angel.* Six years old. Jane's age.

Eliza Ann Bird, 1922–1936. She rests in peace with God. Joseph's sister, one year younger than me.

Other children are here, not just Birds. "People used to have very large families," says Margaret. "Eight, nine, ten children or more. It's because a lot of children died young. It was just the way it was."

I take her hand and she squeezes it.

I could stay here for hours imagining the lives of all these people.

"I'm having a stone made for Jimmy and your mom," says Margaret. "Both their names on the same stone. We'll bury some of their ashes here, and we'll scatter the rest in Aspen Lake."

Jane knows all about ashes. We talked about it again last night when I knew we were coming here.

"Where are the memorial benches?" she says suddenly.

Margaret gazes around. "I don't think—"

"The memorial benches." Jane's voice rises. "There has to be a memorial bench when someone dies."

"We always walk along the seawall in Stanley Park and look at the memorial benches," I explain. "It's our tradition."

"That's a great idea," says Uncle Rob. He's with us again, giving Margaret a long hug. "I'm sure we can find someone here to make us a bench."

"You have to write a saying on it," says Jane.

"You're right," says Margaret. "Maybe you girls could think of something."

"I'll just be a minute," I say.

I go back to Daryl and Daphne's gravesite. I scrape away moss from the stone so that our name stands out clearly. *BIRD.*

I like to think that there's a part of my great-great-grandmother Daphne Bird inside me.

Daryl and Daphne, Joseph and Mary, Wayne and Margaret, Uncle Rob, Uncle Jimmy, and Mom. Me and Jane. And all the others. We're all Birds.

Susan wants to plan a celebration of life for Mom and Uncle Jimmy. She says people in Aspen Lake will want to come. Margaret's not sure if she's ready for that. "Maybe something small," she says.

When it's time to bury the ashes, we'll come back here. I'm afraid of what that might feel like but I'm thankful for one thing. Uncle Jimmy and Mom will be surrounded by Birds.

We're almost home when I know exactly what I want the bench to say.

Because we were twins.

Before I can open my mouth, Jane says, "You know how Uncle Jimmy was Mom's brother?"

"Yes," says Margaret.

"The bench should say 'We loved each other.'"

"What do you think, Rob?" says Margaret.

"I like it. It says it all. And it's poetic, too."

"Rachel?"

I poke Jane in the ribs. "It's pretty good."

Margaret smiles at Jane. "It's perfect."

CHAPTER FIFTY-THREE

If I'm going to keep staring at the ceiling over my bunk every day, I should put something there to stare at.

I know I'm just trying to keep my mind from stressing about Cody. I have no idea when people stop picking up hay bales. Six o'clock? Seven o'clock? Eight o'clock? I'm not even sure what it means.

For some unknown reason, Margaret has a huge supply of sticky tac for attaching things to walls and, in my case, ceilings. I take down the Amnesty International poster from the wall in Mom's room and stick it on the ceiling right above my pillow. Then I arrange all the photos of Mom and Magic barrel racing in a circle around it.

Then I lie on my bunk and stare at it.

Something's not right on the poster. It's the words—the longest row of words that forms the bottom of the pyramid.

The letters are smaller. Not as even. And they're navy blue, not black.

JIMMYASKEDMETODRIVEANDISAIDNO ITSMYFAULTMYFAULTMYFAULT

I separate the words.

JIMMY ASKED ME TO DRIVE AND I SAID NO ITS MY FAULT MY FAULT MY FAULT

I stare at it, shocked.

The photo of Uncle Jimmy beside his car, holding the bottle of beer, came from Mom's camera.

Mom must have taken it. She knew he'd been drinking. Then what happened? He asked her to drive, and she said no.

Why? Was she mad? Was she tired? Or did she just not want to?

I swallow hard. I think she just didn't want to.

Margaret said that Mom was in her room, listening to music on headphones. Maybe that was true. Maybe she thought Uncle Jimmy wouldn't have the nerve to drive himself. But she never told Margaret and Wayne that he had asked her.

Just like I never told anyone that Jane asked *me* to boil water for her Mr. Noodles.

I didn't tell Mrs. Gunty, the social worker, Mom. Not even Aura.

Our kettle was broken, and we had to boil water in a pot with a wobbly handle. I never thought Jane would have the nerve to try it by herself.

I tuck my quilt around me.

Maybe Mom wanted someone to find her message. Maybe she didn't. Who was she writing it for? When did she write it? Last summer, when Uncle Jimmy died, or sixteen years ago just before she left Aspen Lake?

If I leave the poster on the ceiling, one day Jane might figure out Mom's message, too. I'm not sure if I want that. I could take it down, bury it in a cupboard, or tear it up and drop it into the woodstove like I did the photo. It's another thing that Margaret can't see.

I stare at it for a long time.

For now, it stays.

I think about everything that's happened. This is what I work out: When something really bad happens, it happens so fast. You do something, and later you wish with all your heart that you had done something different. You have to decide if you're going to tell someone, and you don't. Then, even if you want to, it's too late.

I think of Margaret, trying to go to the police station. I think of Mom, keeping our family a secret for fifteen years. I think of me, never admitting what I did to Jane.

I'm going to tell Margaret the truth.

This is what I'll say:

After Jane burned herself, I kept having this nightmare where she burns herself, over and over again, and then I got too scared to fall asleep and now I can't.

I'm going to say:

Jane asked me to boil the water for her Mr. Noodles and I was reading, and *I just didn't want to.*

I said no.

CHAPTER FIFTY-FOUR

"Do you ever eat anything besides apples?" says Cody.

I'm hunched over on the top verandah step, concentrating on chewing instead of worrying. I spin around.

"Dad and Samantha brought me over," he says. "They're in the kitchen, talking to Margaret and Rob."

He drops down beside me. "So. What do you want to say to me?"

I take a deep breath. I pour out a garbled story about Uncle Jimmy, my mom, Stephanie, Butterfly Lake, the yurt, the car. I keep saying, *I'm so sorry. I'm so sorry. I'm so sorry.*

"What exactly are you apologizing for?" he says.

I'm drained.

"I don't know."

There's a long, long silence.

Finally I whisper, "Please say something."

"Okay." Cody blows out air. "After Rob left our place, Dad cried. I've never seen him cry before. It was awful."

"Oh God. I am so sorry. I know I keep saying that—"

"It's okay, Rach. Really. Samantha came right away and we talked for hours. Her and me and Dad. At the end Dad said it was going to give him some closure. That's kind of cliché but it's true."

"What about you?"

"It's different for me. I wasn't there. Obviously." He pauses. "Well, technically I was but you know what I mean."

"It's still so hard to believe."

"I know. I feel like this is some nightmare about another kid's life, not mine."

"Me too," I say. "That's exactly how I feel."

Cody flicks a pinecone off the edge of the step. "That *Crime Watchers* show really messed me up. I can't get it out of my head. It's just stupid to keep watching it. It won't change anything. And then seeing my mother on that CD was like a kick in the gut. I probably need some closure too."

"But you were so cool with the CD. I thought—"

"Yeah, well, you're not the only one who hides things, Rachel Bird."

"Who, me?"

We laugh.

It feels good to laugh.

And I'm so glad Cody has told me all this. Because I just didn't know.

"So. Do you want to keep talking about it?" he says.

"Yes. We have to. Definitely. But maybe not right now. Later?"

Cody has sweat marks on his T-shirt. There's a crease on his forehead from his baseball cap.

"Did you know there's hay in your hair?" I say.

"Yeah? Guess how many hay bales I picked up today?"

"Fifty?"

"Two hundred. In the sun. No shade. Fifty pounds each. Forty bales makes one ton of hay. I picked up five tons of hay."

"Wow. Where did you put them?"

"On the hay trailer. And then in the hay shed. And in the winter, they'll go in the horse barn. Not all at once."

Ah. Picking up hay bales. I get it now.

He leans over and we kiss.

"So, let's go swimming," he says.

That I can do.

~

Jane flies into our room. "Rachel! You've been asleep forever! Presents! Come RIGHT NOW!"

I jump down off the bunk.

A big paper shopping bag is sitting on the kitchen table with packages, wrapped in Christmas paper, sticking out the top.

"Uncle Rob brought them," says Margaret.

"They were in your old apartment, in a cupboard," he says.

Jane's bouncing. "Who are they from?"

"Mom," I say.

"Mom!" she says. "Why did we have to wait until now?"

"Because, Jane-O," says Uncle Rob, "I wanted Margaret to be here, too."

Jane has four presents and I have three. Jane loves everything. A stuffed penguin, a play dough kit with plastic molds, a card game called *Moose in the House*, a book about a unicorn. I was with Mom when she bought Jane's presents at a dollar store. Why didn't I wonder what had happened to them?

I unwrap my presents. Three books. *Daughter of the Forest* by Juliet Marillier (brand new), *Daughter of Smoke and Bone* by Laini Taylor (used), and *The Daughter of Time* by Josephine Tey (used). Mom taught me my system for choosing books.

In my next life, I'll come back as a Daughter of the Forest.

"There's something else," says Jane, reaching into the bottom of the shopping bag.

"Let me see."

She passes me what looks like tickets, paper clipped together. There's three of them. I read them and hand them to Margaret.

"What are they?" says Jane.

"Bus tickets," I say. "For last year. December twenty-first. One adult and two youth. They were for you and me and Mom."

"Where were we going to go?"

Margaret's hand is clasped to her mouth.

"Here," I say. "We were going to come here."

~

"I need something to stare at, too," says Jane.

I get the sticky tac and Jane gets the paper and we attach it to the wooden slats under my bunk bed, right over Jane's pillow.

We read it out loud together.

I, Rachel Daphne Bird and I, Jane Mary Bird, do solemnly swear to be best friends forever on pain of death. We seal this with an oath of blood on July 21.

Rachel Daphne Bird
Jane Mary Bird

Witness: Bella

"Did we get enough blood?" says Jane. "I think we should do it again."

CHAPTER FIFTY-FIVE

Amber's here. I make tea, and she and Margaret and I sit at the kitchen table. Amber wants to talk about Stephanie.

She cries and I leave them and go outside. This is about Margaret and Amber. Not me.

I get Magic and tie him to the hitching post. I'm not going to ride. I just want to be with him. I'm brushing his tail when Amber comes out to the car.

She seems okay. She's smiling. She strokes Magic's neck. "Hi, guy."

There's something I need to ask her. "Amber?"

"Yeah."

"What's happening about selling the ranch?"

"Oh that," she says. "It's just not important anymore."

~

Margaret and I are sitting under the ancient fir tree. The grassy slope is gouged with ATV tracks and black mud is churned into hills and valleys.

Margaret's telling me about prom night.

"Wayne let them take his truck to Hundred Mile. It was three o'clock in the morning when they got home. I remember because I could never sleep when they were out. Jimmy went off to the yurt, but your mom was way too excited to go to bed. She wanted to tell me everything. They'd all gone to the prom together. Your mom, Jimmy, Jesse, Stephanie, and Amber. They were always in a group. Always having fun."

"What did Mom wear?"

"A beautiful blue dress. It went right to the floor. All the girls wore long dresses to their proms. I don't know if they still do."

"I'm not sure." I can't imagine my prom. I don't even know if I'd want to go.

"It was very hard for Stephanie to find a dress that fit," says Margaret. "She was almost seven months pregnant. They just didn't make prom dresses for pregnant girls. But your mom was determined. There was nothing in Hundred Mile, so they went to Kamloops."

"Did Amber go, too?"

"Oh yes. Your mom always made sure that Amber wasn't left out. Your mom and Amber found their dresses first, and then they talked Stephanie into a red dress that was quite tight. You could even call it slinky. The girls modeled their dresses when they got back. They looked absolutely gorgeous."

Margaret smiles. "And Jimmy, too. He was so handsome that night. Just like his father."

The silver ribbon of water digs a channel through the mud, on its way to Aspen Lake.

"I wish the beavers were still here," I say.

"They'll come back," says Margaret. "They're attracted to the sound of running water."

Will I be here long enough to see a new Butterfly Lake? I hope so. Uncle Rob's going to stay for the whole month of August. He's going to take over for a while, and I'm totally good with that. His first priorities are to look for more help for the ranch and take the yurt down. What happens next depends on whether Wayne is charged with a crime. The lawyer's coming tomorrow night. We'll know more then.

If it's possible, at the beginning of September, Uncle Rob might make a trip to Poland. But he'll come right back.

So what about me and Jane? Uncle Rob's promised that we'll come up with a plan together. He says the news is going to spread fast in Aspen Lake, that people are basically kind here, but there will definitely be gossip and that might be hard for us.

We'll deal with it. We're in this together, me, Jane, Uncle Rob, Margaret, and Wayne.

"We should get back to the house," says Margaret. "I've promised Jane that she can have Cassie over to play today."

Before I go, I search for the bald eagle in his tower and in the hazy sky. The King of Butterfly Lake has left.

Maybe, just maybe, we don't need him anymore.

~

I squeeze my legs against Magic's sides. He breaks into a trot, then a lope. Dancer's hooves are thudding behind me.

We're in an open field, full of blowing daisies.

Margaret and I gallop side by side, the wind in our faces.

CHAPTER FIFTY-SIX

We're in the pea patch in the garden. Margaret shows us how to tell if a pea pod is ready for picking.

If it's flat, leave it. If the peas are bulging out, it's too late and you can toss it to Bella.

The perfect pea pod is in between, not thin, not fat.

I carry the sack of pea pods to the table on the verandah. Margaret brings out a large bowl and a piece of newspaper to put the empty pods on. The best way to do this, she explains, is to slice the pod open with your fingernail and then use your index finger to slide the peas into the bowl.

It's not as easy as it sounds. Peas escape, bouncing on the table and rolling onto the floor. Bella lunges for them. Jane eats more peas than she puts in the bowl. Our fingers turn green.

"There's a rhythm to shelling peas," says Margaret. "Sometimes it feels like a ritual. A summer ritual."

We don't talk, not even Jane. The only sound is the *plink* of the peas in the bowl.

∿

"I'm going to call Margaret Grandma," says Jane.

"That's not very original," I say. "It's boring."

She screws up her face. She's got her thinking cap on.

"Can I make a suggestion?"

"What?"

"Nana."

"Nana? Why?"

"Because," I say, "Nana is the kind of grandmother who gives names to ducks in a park. Margaret would do that, too."

"Okay," says Jane. "What should Wayne's name be?"

"Papa, I think. Nana and Papa. That sounds good together."

Jane's using felt pens to make a card for Wayne. She writes *Papa* in fluorescent pink.

As for me, I'm going to keep saying Margaret and Wayne. I'm fifteen. Too old to change.

∿

Wayne's coming home next week. I'm going to tell him I'll type his book.

~

I'm in the hammock with Cody.

We're comparing legs. His are tanned super dark. His calves are very muscular. He says my legs are pale beige. I correct him. Pale bronze.

"I've decided on my tattoo," I say. "Finally."

"Yeah? What's it going to be?"

"A *draumstafir*."

"Oh good. That's harder to say than the other one."

I punch his arm. "I found it in the Huld Manuscript. It's a sleep symbol. It looks kind of like a staff with swirly lines. You're supposed to scratch it on silver or white leather on St. John's Night, and then when the sun is at its lowest, you'll sleep all night, and you'll dream whatever you want to dream. It's perfect for me."

"Where are you going to get—?"

"WHOOOHOWHOOOHOOHOO...."

Uh-oh.

"I'M RIIIISING FROM THE DEEEEP...," says Jane.

Cody and I hit the ground with a THUMP!

"After her!" yells Cody.

Jane screams. She's fast, like a rabbit.

I'm faster.

CHAPTER FIFTY-SEVEN

I'm in Mom's room, sitting at her desk. I'm making a white butterfly.

Rotate the paper ninety degrees clockwise.
Turn the model over.
Valley fold the bottom edge to the top.

I know what a valley fold is now. I know all the vocabulary. Squash fold. Mountain fold. Inside-reverse fold.

Your butterfly should look like this.

It does. It's beautiful.
Perched on the edge of the desk, it's ready to soar. I make a second butterfly. It's beautiful, too.

I write a name on one wing of each butterfly.

Jimmy.
Layla.

I'm going to hang them in the butterfly house, beside Stephanie's butterfly. But not yet. I want my whole family to be here. Uncle Rob, Margaret, Jane.
And Wayne. I'll wait for Wayne.
Then I'll show Cody.

~

JANE'S ~~NEW~~ ~~NEW~~ NEW FAVORITE FOODS
Chocolate Lucky Charms
Homemade pizza
Carrots from the garden
Strawberries from the garden
Raspberries from the garden
Cucumbers from the garden
Nana's chicken pot pie
Nana's meatloaf
Yam fries
Beans from the garden
Saskatoon berry pie
Poutine
Peanut butter cookies
Viva Puffs
Peas from the garden

~

THREE BARS IN MY BUNK BED!!!
IT'S A MIRACLE!!!!!

~

ME: So what's in Manitoba?

JASON: BILLIONS of stars.

~

ME: Jane says an Aldabra giant tortoise lived to
225 years old in a zoo in India. That's a point in
favor of a carapace.

AURA: Who wants to live to 225? All your friends
will be dead.

~

AMBER: Riding on Saturday?

ME: Yes!!!

~

CODY: Hey

ME: Hey

~

I get Jane, and we go to the lake. This time, instead of the trail through the trees, we wander through the field. The grass is as tall as Jane. She's making bead necklaces now, and we're both adorned with three necklaces and an armful of bracelets. I grab her hand and we run. Bella bounds ahead, barking.

There's so much I don't know. I don't know when Jane will stop wetting her bed and when I'll sleep right through the night. I don't know if Cody and I will fall in love. I don't know if Wayne will go to prison or even if he should. I don't know if Aleksandra will come back or if Uncle Rob will go to Poland. I still don't even know for sure if we'll be living in Aspen Lake in September.

But I do know this.

I don't want to be the Daughter of the Forest. I don't want to live in Hope, in the Palace of Versailles, or in Tajikistan. I don't want to be Bella or a pioneer or a mermaid. I don't want to be Lady Smoke.

In my next life, I'll be Rachel Bird.

THE END

ACKNOWLEDGMENTS

A heartfelt thank you to the amazing team at Second Story Press and to my editor, Heather Tekavec, whose invaluable suggestions pointed me in the right direction.

I would like to thank Renée Hall, who invited me to spend an interesting afternoon with her in a yurt on Salt Spring Island, and Derek Chambers for a very enjoyable couple of hours in his studio in Bridge Lake creating my publicity photograph.

My daughter, Meghan, is always a huge inspiration and source of ideas for my writing. Her love of mythology, symbolism, and all things mystical (and her tattoo of a Viking compass!) became an important part of Rachel.

This book would never have been written without the incredible commitment of my sister, Janet. She read and reread the many drafts in between long sessions of brainstorming.

She often came up with the missing detail that made each scene or piece of dialogue stronger.

My life on our ranch with my husband, Larry, and Meghan is reflected throughout Rachel's story. I can't thank Larry enough for looking after everything so well and making it possible for me to have the time to write.

ABOUT THE AUTHOR

BECKY CITRA is the author of 23 award-winning books for children. She lives on a ranch in British Columbia. She spends the winters on Salt Spring Island. A retired school teacher, she enjoys connecting with children through library and school visits.